DESIGNS ON A DUKE

THE BLUESTOCKING SCANDALS
BOOK ONE

ELLIE ST. CLAIR

CONTENTS

Facebook: Ellie St. Clair

Cover by AJF Designs

Do you love historical romance? Receive access to a free ebook, as well as exclusive content such as giveaways, contests, freebies and advance notice of pre-orders through my mailing list!

Sign up here!

Also By Ellie St. Clair

The Bluestocking Scandals
Designs on a Duke
Inventing the Viscount
Discovering the Baron
The Valet Experiment
Writing the Rake
Risking the Detective
A Noble Excavation
A Gentleman of Mystery

The Bluestocking Scandals Box Set: Books 1-4
The Bluestocking Scandals Box Set: Books 5-8

For a full list of all of Ellie's books, please see
www.elliestclair.com/books.

CHAPTER 1

LONDON ~ 1820

*T*he door knocker appeared to be frowning.

Rebecca tilted her head to better study the gigantic lion that stared her in the eye. This one was quite stoic and serious, its eyebrows narrowed in anger and, perhaps, a bit of worry. If the duke was attempting to discourage visitors, then he was certainly achieving his purpose.

"A door knocker should be welcoming, should it not?" she asked her father, who was making his own study of the front exterior of the house.

"It's a shame, really," he murmured, looking around. "A house of this size, in the middle of London, kept secret from all eyes for years now. Look at the gardens on the southern side! But Becca, this house… why it's not finished!"

"You're right," she said, her eyes widening. From afar it looked rather extravagant, but upon closer examination, all of the finishing details had not yet been completed. "We shall see what the interior holds. But Father, let's not tell him any of our thoughts on his home until we further determine just why he has asked us here."

"He quite obviously wants to hire us!" her father exclaimed indignantly. "I am in high demand, Becca. High demand! I have heard much of Wyndham House, you know. There were plans for it to be rather grand, but there is no need to determine just why it wasn't completed, for it is quite obvious. Clearly the initial design was flawed. The duke must know that I will *not* simply follow another's designs."

"Father, we need this commission," Rebecca said, tapping her foot nervously, hoping that her father would move on from his passionate criticism of what could be one of the grandest mansions in London.

All knew of Wyndham House, as it covered one of the largest footprints of any home in the city. But its fame was partially hinged on the fact that it had become something of a mystery.

It was nearly a decade now since the first brick had been laid, but for the past eight years, no one besides servants had set foot in it. The recently passed duke had been quite ill during his final years, and his visitors consisted solely of caretakers as he had no immediate relatives.

Which was partially why the dukedom had passed into the hands of this man, a far-removed cousin, who apparently had been unaware that he would someday become one of the most powerful men in England.

It was all quite intriguing. But Rebecca was intent on dismissing all of the gossip and fascination that surrounded the new duke and focusing on the task at hand. It would take all of her concentration to do so.

She took a deep breath as the door swung open.

"Good morning," said the man Rebecca assumed to be the

butler, though he was much younger than any butler she had ever met.

He was tall, handsome in a boyish way, and had a spark in his eye as he looked Rebecca up and down before turning his gaze onto her father.

"You must be Mr. Lambert," he said. "I am Dexter. Do come in."

Rebecca and her father stepped into the foyer, both of them immediately more interested in their surroundings than any of the human inhabitants.

The foyer was designed to impress but was lacking the details of a completed room. A dome in the ceiling had yet to be ornamented, and Rebecca thought that a gold inlay would make it sparkle like the sun. Perhaps with diamonds. There were cutouts in the wall for statues, the arched doorway beyond providing a glimpse of a grand staircase. How much better would it look, Rebecca mused, to be rid of the wall and have the staircase greet the arrivals? Something worth a discussion.

When they had finally finished their initial review as Dexter waited patiently, the three of them stood staring at one another.

"Is, ah, the duke in residence?" Rebecca finally asked. The butler, who stood before them, was unexpectedly hesitant.

"That's just the thing, Miss..."

"Lambert. Mr. Lambert is my father."

"Ah, yes, Miss Lambert. The duke was supposed to be here to meet you, but has not yet returned home."

"I see," Rebecca said, though, in truth, she was rather annoyed. So the new duke, despite his supposedly common upbringing, had already become like the rest of the nobility. "Shall we wait?"

"Of course," he said, though he made no move to show them into the house.

"Is the drawing room available?" she suggested with a raised eyebrow.

The butler looked rather flustered.

"Perhaps the parlor would be better."

"Very well," Rebecca said, willing patience.

So they were to be relegated to the parlor. Apparently they were not fine enough quality to be shown to the drawing room.

It was likely under the duke's own instructions. Rebecca had been around more than her fair share of the nobility as she had spent her life following her father from one commission to another. In some homes they were seen as upper servants, though her father had gained much respect over the years, the better his name became known. *She* was most often looked right through, seen almost like furniture.

"You see, Becca?" she heard her father murmur in her ear. "Unfinished. Ragged. Shameful."

He was right on the first two accounts. Despite the fact the house had been standing for a decade, many of the walls were bare, unadorned, some of the ceilings half-painted. Draperies covered some windows but not others, and furniture that had been accumulated had the look of that which was to have bided time until new furniture was procured.

That day had obviously not yet come.

They passed through the foyer and then into a long chamber that Rebecca guessed was to be a ballroom. It was currently empty except for two long tables, upon which sat a curious collection of objects.

She was so busy looking at their contents that she walked right into her father, who had stopped to stare at everything in front of him.

"What in the…"

"Father," Rebecca warned, cutting him off. Just then a jar

of green liquid on the table began to bubble, and Rebecca took a step backward, pulling her father with her.

Just as it exploded with white foam shooting out the top of the jar, a tall, slim woman dressed in green raced into the room.

"I'm so sorry," she said, clearly flustered as she attempted to push back some of the strands of blonde hair that floated around her face, though she refrained from touching her skin with her gloved hands. "I didn't know we were having company and I should have had this in another room. That being said, I think I am close to—"

"Jemima!"

"Oh, Mother!" the woman whirled around as an elegantly dressed white-haired woman *sailed* into the room — Rebecca didn't think walked was an adequate description. A strong floral scent wafted around her like a cloud.

"Hello there," she said, waving a hand in front of her demurely, giving Rebecca the idea that the woman hailed herself near to royal status — which, Rebecca supposed, she now was, as the immediate family of a duke. "You must be the architect. Please, do wait in the parlor. We look forward to our discussion. Dexter, please show them in. And next time, perhaps walk them the other way, through the drawing room?"

"Very well, Mrs. St. Vincent," he said with the slightest of bows and he waved a hand in the air, bidding them to continue to follow him.

Rebecca and her father exchanged a look, but Rebecca shrugged and urged her father to continue, though they both jumped at the bang that exploded from the table behind them.

"Sorry," the younger woman — Miss St. Vincent— said with a cringe and a bit of a wave before she returned to her work.

"How very curious," Rebecca's father murmured as they finally entered the parlor.

While this room, too, was not yet complete, Rebecca was drawn to the large Venetian window on the far wall, which overlooked the back court. A huge green expanse flourished beyond, though there was much potential to expand the gardens. This should be the focal point of the room, Rebecca thought. The furniture should look out beyond the window, the remainder of the room simple and unornamented.

The door opened behind them, and Rebecca turned, hoping to see the duke so they could be on with it, but instead it was the woman she assumed to be his mother.

"Wonderful to meet you, Mr. Lambert," she said with a wide, practiced smile on her face, as though they had not just encountered one another in the ballroom. She took a seat in one of the mismatched chairs, this one a royal-blue upholstered mahogany one that had been home to many bottoms, artfully arranging her expansive, clearly expensive, skirts over the chair so they fanned out evenly. "I am Mrs. St. Vincent and my son is the Duke of Wyndham."

"A pleasure to meet you," Rebecca's father said, his practiced charm emerging as he bent to kiss the woman's hand, though she pulled it away before he was able to do so.

"Yes, well. My son was supposed to be here to meet you, but unfortunately, he was called away on very *urgent* matters. As you may know, we have only recently arrived at this home in London, and as you can see, there is much to complete. I know my son has more particulars in mind and will review them once he arrives, but obviously the house has the potential to be *quite* opulent."

"Actually, Mrs. St. Vincent, we haven't seen much of it," Rebecca said, growing rather impatient. They hadn't much time to waste waiting. "Perhaps while we wait, we could tour the house?"

"And you are...?" she asked, fixing her pointed stare on Rebecca.

"Miss Lambert. I assist my father as his secretary."

"Oh. How unusual. Well. I suppose Dexter can show you around, if you must see it now."

They rose and Rebecca followed her father out. He began chattering away in Dexter's ear, and Rebecca followed behind, pulling out her sketchbook and making notes as well as drawing sketches and designs as she went.

The style was Palladian with a hint of neoclassical, she realized as they wandered through, and she wished she was able to better question the duke as to what had happened over the past decade. At least the current duke was willing to pay for additional work. While her father may have blamed shoddy design, the truth was evident. The previous duke had run out of money.

She poked her head into one room and then the other. It was a travesty, really, and Rebecca wondered what the country estate looked like. Stripped of all its finery, perhaps, in order to attempt to pay to keep up appearances? No wonder this place remained a mystery.

She stopped for a moment, attempting a quick drawing, when suddenly she realized how quiet the hall had become. Rebecca looked up to find that her father and Dexter were nowhere in sight. Drat. She had become too caught up.

She quickly ascended the staircase in an attempt to catch them, but the upstairs corridor was empty as well. Rebecca put her ear against one door and then the next, but there was no sign of them. There was, however, a door slightly ajar at the end of the hall. She continued toward it, pushing it fully open to reveal a long, wide bedchamber. The windows were covered in heavy navy draperies, the bed itself taking up a large portion of the room. Goodness, how large was the duke that he needed such space?

Curious, Rebecca walked further into the room, though she was aware that this was likely not one of the rooms Dexter would have included in his tour. But she couldn't help herself. She loved studying how people lived. And, unlike many rooms in the house, this chamber was obviously occupied.

There was a small dressing room and another door that Rebecca assumed connected to another bedroom. She pushed it open, finding the bedroom entirely bare. So there was clearly no *her* grace. Rebecca was about to retreat when she heard a heavy tread in the hallway, the steps coming closer and finally entering the room.

Not the wandering, unhurried steps of her father. Not the quick steps of Dexter.

It must be the duke.

Her heart began to race at the thought of being caught in the bedchamber of one of the highest peers in all of England. How would she ever explain herself? Rebecca did the first thing that came into her mind.

She hid.

CHAPTER 2

alentine St. Vincent, the sixth Duke of Wyndham, was tired.

He was tired of balls. He was tired of operas. He was tired of pretending to be the Duke of Wyndham when all he had ever aspired to be was a man making a name for himself in his chosen profession, which was the only thing he truly excelled at. One who would be perfectly happy spending his life without any pressure or great responsibility placed upon him.

But then his brother had died. His father had died. His cousin was deemed illegitimate. And then the old duke had finally succumbed to the illness that had kept him bedridden for years, and Val remained the fortuitous one to be alive and declared the duke after a lengthy inquiry by the College of Arms.

He let himself into his house — though it was styled more of a mansion than anything else, and finding his butler utterly absent, he hung his hat up himself.

A crash resounded from down the hall and he smiled to himself. Jemima. At least some things never changed. His sister was still as curious in unraveling the next great scientific discovery. He didn't understand half of it, though she was always more than pleased to provide a running commentary of her most recent hypothesis. Currently, it was something to do with the effects of the cleanliness — or lack thereof — of water.

He strode through the foyer to what was supposed to be a ballroom but had become Jemima's laboratory. He found her blonde head bent over a microscope, so focused that she didn't even look up when he walked into the room.

"Good to see you haven't destroyed our new home quite yet," he said, and she yelped as she jumped up.

"Val! You scared me."

He chuckled as he tapped a hand against his leg, where an old injury still aggravated him from time to time.

"Where is everyone?"

"Hmm?"

Her mind was still elsewhere.

"Dexter wasn't at the door. Usually he is so eager to prove himself as a new butler that I can hardly untie my own cloak."

"Dexter? Oh yes, he came through here not long ago."

"Jem?" He tried not to sigh in exasperation, but he only needed a moment of her time.

"Right. Ummm, he had some people with him. I think they went into the parlor. So did Mother."

She waved her hand toward the end of the room, where the parlor was located.

"People? Oh, right — the architect." He slapped a hand to his forehead. "I completely forgot."

"And you call me absentminded."

When she finally looked up at him, her eyes widened and she snorted.

"You certainly cannot greet them looking like that."

"Why not?"

"You look as though someone just gave you a sound pummeling."

"I actually came out the victor, thank you very much."

He looked down at himself and saw that his sister had a point.

She was shaking her head now.

"I really don't understand why you continue to go back to Jackson's."

He walked over to the table and tweaked her nose as though she was still a girl and not a woman over twenty.

"And I don't understand why you enjoy mixing your liquids in here all day, but I leave you be, don't I?"

"Fair point."

"Very well. I best wash up and then I'll meet with the architect. Though I wish Mother hadn't pressured me into hiring one. We have no money to pay for him."

"That's why you're supposed to marry someone wealthy," Jemima said absently, returning to her work, apparently dismissing him.

Val sighed as he found the stairs and began to trudge up to his room. Truth be told, the only joy he could find in his current life was through some physical activity and boxing served the dual purpose of keeping up his strength as well as releasing the tension that seemed to build as he sat at his damned desk all day working in the ledgers the old duke had left. Val had fired his man of business who had supposedly handled everything but truly bungled it all. Val was determined to figure this out on his own before he trusted another to look after things for him.

He entered the large ducal suite, aware that it was too depressing, too dismal. It made him feel as though he was living in some remote Scottish castle. He'd have the architect take a look at this room, see if there was anything to be done.

Although his sister had said that *architects* had arrived — he only recalled asking one to come to consult with him. He certainly couldn't afford two. Hopefully the man had simply brought an assistant.

He stripped off his bloody shirt and threw it on the bed, realizing as he did so that he had forgotten to call for the valet, and Dexter wouldn't know to tell Archie he had returned. Well, soon enough, word would get round that he was home and Archie would be through the bedroom door and ready to offer him his assistance as well as his commentary.

He was not the most conventional of servants, but he was one of the few not constantly awaiting his every command, which was beginning to unnerve him.

Well, until Archie arrived, he supposed he could select his own clothes.

He opened the door to his dressing room, reaching out a hand as he did — and touched something very soft, very silky, and very smooth.

"Who's there?" he demanded, opening the door wider to allow more light in.

There stood a woman, her greenish-brown eyes wide as they stared at him over a pert nose. Her jet black hair was pulled back from her head, seemingly long and straight as pieces tumbled down from the pins over her back. What he couldn't tear his eyes away from? Those cherry-red lips, just begging to be kissed. They parted now, as though she was about to say something, but just then he heard a sound from the corridor.

"Your grace?"

Not Archie. Dexter.

For a moment, Val forgot that he was a duke, that he had no one to answer to but himself. He went back to being a young man, who was frightened of his father discovering any transgression. Before he could even think of what he was doing, he stepped into the dressing room, nearly pressing himself against the woman, and shut the door behind him.

* * *

REBECCA STOOD SO STILL in shock that she had no idea what she was supposed to do next. She was an intelligent woman. She should have a witty response on the tip of her tongue.

But inspiration had never come quickly to her. Rather, she had to stew on something, turn it over in her mind until just the right thought entered and answered her current problem.

"Ah... you must be the Duke of Wyndham," she finally managed before sensing movement. "Did you just nod?"

"I did," he said, his voice deeper, rougher than she had expected. "My apologies. Rather idiotic of me. Yes, I am the Duke of Wyndham."

"Well, I cannot say this is how I thought I would make your acquaintance."

"Rather silly for us to be hiding in here," he said with the slightest of chuckles. "I, ah, saw a beautiful woman, heard a voice in the hall, and acted on instinct."

"To hide with a woman?" she asked, pleased that he couldn't see the flush in her cheeks at being called beautiful.

"Err..."

"You don't need to answer that," she said quickly. What had gotten into her?

But then he laughed. His laugh was a low rumble that began deep in his chest before resounding throughout the dressing chamber. It was one of those laughs that was so contagious, one had no choice but to join in.

And so she did. It was freeing, chasing away both the

awkwardness for a moment and the need for either of them to say anything within this strange encounter.

"I think he's gone now," the duke said after their laughter subsided, and sure enough, the sounds of his butler calling out "Your grace?" was no longer. "Poor Dexter. He will be most distressed. At least he likely found my shirt to take to the valet for laundering. That should keep him busy for a time."

"Your shirt?"

"Yes, it had some... stains."

"I see."

Rebecca was quite confused by this entire encounter, but who was she to question a duke?

"I, ah, best be going now," she said, slowly inching around him, doing all she could to not slide her body over his as she sought the door. Relief swept over her when she found the handle, and she turned the knob open, allowing light to enter once more though she didn't look back. "I shall see you in the parlor," she managed, before slipping out the door and nearly running out of the bedroom, along the corridor, and down the stairs.

* * *

VALENTINE STOOD THERE IN SHOCK, staring after the beauty. One look at her and he had turned into a blithering fool.

It was this entire new situation, he told himself. He was having a difficult time learning how he was supposed to interact with his peers, his servants, and... whoever this woman was. As she had escaped his room so quickly that he nearly wondered if she had seen a mouse, he realized that he had no idea who she was or what she was doing in his bedchamber. Apparently not a gift, he realized with a rueful laugh.

He was right in that his soiled shirt had been taken away, but he knew it would take him a great deal longer to dress himself than with the help of his valet. With company about he was expected, as a duke, to always be fully dressed in a waistcoat and cravat, as uncomfortable as they were. He walked to the door, throwing it open.

"Archie!" he bellowed, but instead of seeing his valet approach, a tall, distinguished gentleman he had never seen before was wandering down his corridor. What in the...

"Hello, sir," the man said, "to what do I owe the pleasure?"

"Ah... I'm not entirely sure," Val said, scratching his hair, which had been cut fairly short upon his arrival in London. He missed his usual longer locks. "Just who are you?"

"Why, I am Albert Lambert, of course."

"Lambert — the architect. Right," Val said, frowning. What kind of architect had he hired? "I thought you were awaiting me in the parlor."

"The parlor? We finished the parlor weeks ago!" Lambert said, further confusing Val. "We must now continue with the ballroom."

"That will be the last of it," Val said. "We must make sure we build my sister a proper laboratory first."

"Laboratory?" the man repeated back to him, a frown marring his face. "I wasn't told of a laboratory."

"Yes, well, I will explain everything when we discuss the project further," Val said, relieved when he saw Archie approaching down the hall. "I will be down to meet with you shortly, Mr. Lambert. My apologies for my tardiness."

He stepped back into the room, Archie following him with a questioning look, as Mr. Lambert nodded and strode away in the other direction.

My, but this was a strange day.

CHAPTER 3

*R*ebecca tapped her foot as the duke finally entered the room and took a seat next to his mother. The four of them now — finally — sat around the small table in the middle of the room, the duke and his mother in mismatched chairs, Rebecca and her father on a worn sofa across from them.

She looked up, catching the duke's eye, and he quirked an eyebrow at her, causing a bit of heat to rise in her cheeks.

Her quick glimpse of him before he had entered the dressing room and shut the door behind him, encasing them in darkness, had primarily been directed at his chest, which had lain bare before her eyes.

To be fair, Rebecca hadn't seen many men without clothing on. But she knew much of architectural planes and lines, of exquisite sculptures and works of art.

Which this man was.

From his chiseled shoulders down his bulging biceps, back to his chest which seemed as though it had been etched in granite, he was a vision. She had no idea what he did to achieve such physique, but had she been asked, she would have suggested he continue it.

Now she had a much better view of his face. He was blond, like his sister, though his hair was a darker shade than hers. His dark-blue eyes were deep set, his nose prominent, but unnaturally so. Rebecca guessed that it had been broken a time or two. She assumed some might say it detracted from his looks, but she had always been attracted to the unconventional — the anomalies in stone, the façade that didn't quite fit the rest of the neighborhood, the ability to bring the natural world indoors, with all of its unique qualities.

His lips, which reminded her of a man who smiled often, quirked once more, reminding her of the secret they shared.

"Valentine, how lovely of you to join us," his mother said, her smile wide as she placed a hand on his arm when he took a chair next to her. "I know how busy you are with all of your *ducal* responsibilities."

"That was no excuse to keep Mr. Lambert waiting. And… I am not sure I caught your name," he said, meeting Rebecca's eye. She pursed her lips to keep from smiling once again at his nonchalance.

"I am Rebecca Lambert," she introduced herself. "I assist my father with secretarial duties. Taking notes and that type of thing."

She lifted her notebook and pencil to show him.

"Very good," he said with a nod. "Thank you for coming, Mr. Lambert. I apologize for our fleeting meeting upstairs."

Rebecca's heart stopped. The duke had encountered her father? She looked back and forth between them for a sign that anything was amiss. He and Dexter had finally reconvened with her in the parlor and the butler had seemed rather flustered. She wasn't entirely sure what had happened, though her father had looked around the room with some confusion.

"I thought we had finished this already," he had murmured before she had looked him in the eye and quietly reminded him of why they were there. Recognition had quickly returned, and she had smiled at him encouragingly, though she remained somewhat concerned.

"All is well," her father said simply, and Rebecca sighed in relief, though her shoulders remained tight and she hoped they could finish the meeting quickly, in case her father's memory fled once more.

Rebecca opened the sketch pad so that it would seem that there was a reason as to why she was the one asking questions.

"Now, your grace, what can we do for you?"

"As you can see," he said, waving a hand around the room, "this house is…"

"A travesty!" Rebecca's father said, a finger in the air.

Rebecca tried to inconspicuously bring his hand down.

"Ah, yes," the duke said with a short bark of laughter. "It is, in a way."

"*But* we would like you to return it to all of its glory!" Mrs. St. Vincent exclaimed, as prone to pronouncements as Rebecca's father seemingly was.

"Er, yes," the duke said with a quirk of his lips as Dexter re-entered the room and passed him a roll of papers. "We have the plans from the original architect—"

"Not needed!" Rebecca's father said, shaking his hand in front of him. "I do not work from the plans of another."

"But, perhaps, it would be helpful, Father, for you to have the originals," Rebecca said softly. "Then you can see what was done in the past."

She placed a hand on his knee and looked at him intently.

"Very well," he said with an exaggerated sigh.

Rebecca's father had long had a flair for the dramatic. It was part of what made him the renowned genius he was, but in the past, his bit of theatrics had lost him more than one commission.

The duke laid out the plans on the table before them.

"Everything is here," he said. "The previous duke, well, he was quite ill. Before that, I believe he lost most of his fortune."

"Valentine!" Mrs. St. Vincent admonished him, obviously not pleased he had shared such information with commoners.

"Well, it is true," he said with a shrug. "Mr. Lambert should know what will be ahead of him here."

"Do you, your grace, have the funds to pay for my services?" Rebecca's father asked. Rebecca stilled for a moment. Her father was sometimes *too* direct, although she understood his question. If the duke couldn't afford to pay them, there was no reason for them to be there. They no longer primarily worked for fame or for renown. They worked to stay financially afloat.

"I do," the duke said, though Rebecca caught his hesitation. "For a time, anyway."

"Valentine will be married soon!" Mrs. St. Vincent said, clapping her hands together in glee. "His new wife will bring with her a dowry that will pay for the rest of your work while the duke puts all of his holdings in order. Isn't that right, Valentine?"

Rebecca's eyes flew to the duke. She should have known a man like him — a good-looking young duke — would not be a single man for long. Why it mattered, she had no idea. Yes, she was attracted to him, but that meant nothing. Likely every woman who became acquainted with him was attracted to him. He was a duke and a young, handsome one at that. She was the daughter of an architect and, besides, she had much more important issues to currently be concerned with.

Like that which was before her.

"Congratulations, your grace," she murmured, but he was already shaking his head.

"Nothing has been decided and I do not currently *have* a betrothed," he said with a pointed look at his mother. "My mother is a bit... excited."

Mrs. St. Vincent looked slightly admonished, but she shrugged.

"You will very soon, I am sure."

"So you would like us to finish the details of the mansion?" Rebecca asked.

"Yes," he said before his mother cut in.

"In addition to the furnishings. And then there is the country estate."

"Ah, Mother, I'm not sure..."

"It needs *significant* refurbishment," she said, which the duke shrugged at as though he agreed, despite the somewhat pained expression that crossed his face.

"What I would like are some modernizations," he said, and Rebecca felt her father stiffen beside her now.

"Modernizations?" her father asked. "Would that not ruin the character of the house?"

"Nothing extravagant," the duke said, leaning forward. "I would be interested in perhaps a water closet with drainage."

"There *is* the potential," Rebecca said, forgetting herself for a moment as she tapped her pencil upon her lips. "Though it can be tricky within an existing building."

"You must work quite closely with your father," the duke said, eyeing her intently, and Rebecca placed her pencil back on the paper, attempting nonchalance.

"I do. Forgive me, Father, I became ahead of myself."

"Why not this?" the duke suggested. "Perhaps we do a tour of the house — together this time — and I will review everything that we need. You can provide me with an idea of what the cost will be, and I will tell you what I am able to spend. We will do so here and then continue on to the country estate. But first, I need to know, are you interested? Will you take on the work?"

"You come *very* highly recommended, Mr. Lambert," Mrs. St. Vincent said, folding her hands in her lap. "Lady Alberta told me of all you did for their family's home, and I just *knew* that you would be the best one to help us."

"Thank you," Rebecca's father said. Modesty was one quality he most certainly was *not* known for. "Rebecca and I greatly enjoyed our time with their family. We stayed at their estate to oversee the work."

"Oh, I wasn't aware that you did so."

"Some do not," he said, turning to her, his regality rivaling hers. "I, however, must ensure that everything I design is completed exactly as I imagine it. Isn't that right, Rebecca?"

"Yes, Father," she murmured.

"Well, we will ensure you have all you need," Mrs. St. Vincent said. "Won't we, Valentine?"

"Of course, Mother," he said, though he hadn't removed his gaze from Rebecca, which was causing tingles to run through her entire body. Oh, this wouldn't do. This wouldn't do at all.

"We should be going," she said, jumping up quickly, despite the stares from the others in the room. Suddenly, however, she could hardly breathe with the duke's proximity and she sensed the need to be out of this room and away from his as quickly as possible.

"So soon?" the duke asked, and his mother must have heard something in his tone, for she turned to him with a sharp look.

"I am sure Mr. Lambert is eager to get to work," she said, looking to Rebecca's father, who seemed somewhat perturbed.

"Well, I'm not entirely sure—"

"How long it will take, but we will be sure to send you a note," Rebecca cut him off. He was a proud man, but at the moment there was far more at stake than his pride. If he wasn't careful, he would lose his legacy entirely. "Thank you for your hospitality."

They passed through the ballroom-turned-laboratory on their way out of the mansion, though the duke's sister seemed too engrossed in what she was doing to pay any attention to them. She gave a brief wave as she measured something out in front of her, and the moment they passed through the room they heard her give a shout of glee.

Mrs. St. Vincent pretended nothing had occurred, while the duke chuckled under his breath, though loud enough that Rebecca could hear him. It did show strength of his character that he didn't feel the need to hide his sister's eccentrics. Rebecca wasn't exactly the conventional lady herself, so she understood the importance of working without judgment.

Dexter fetched their cloaks and, for the briefest of moments, the duke brought his hand to the small of Rebecca's back. The heat of his touch scorched through her gown, and a tremor ran through her. Then it was gone and she was left bereft.

"You will be in touch then?" he asked, and Rebecca was about to respond when she saw he was looking at her father — as he should be.

"I will," her father said with a nod. "Farewell, your grace."

And as they walked down the drive toward the massive gate holding all back from Wyndham House, it took everything within Rebecca not to turn around and search him out once more.

He was not the man for her. She had best remember it.

CHAPTER 4

"*H*urry, children, we are going to be late!"

Valentine and Jemima exchanged looks of shared misery as they each took a sip of brandy to fortify themselves.

"Do you suppose there are any other dukes referred to as 'child' by their mothers?" Valentine asked dryly, and his sister laughed.

"Do you think if we sit here and say nothing, she will go without us?" Jemima asked hopefully, but Valentine shook his head.

"Never. She's relentless."

"She wasn't in the past," Jemima said grimly. "Not about us, at any rate."

"No," Valentine said abruptly, all humor vanished, not caring to speak of their older brother at the moment. "She wasn't."

But things had changed. Everything had changed when Matthew was killed.

"Valentine! Jemima! Where in the name of— oh, there you are."

"She found us," Jemima sighed as their mother walked in the door.

"She was bound to eventually," Valentine said out of the corner of his mouth. "Hurry and finish your drink. Let's get this over with."

Jemima downed the brandy in one gulp, impressing Valentine who quickly followed her, though he couldn't help but grimace. His sister was apparently much heartier.

"When was the last time you were at Almack's, Val?" Jemima asked as they donned their cloaks.

"Ages ago," he said, careful with his words as his mother was within hearing. "After the one time, I decided never to go again."

"Matthew would have loved Almack's," their mother said miserably. It had been a few years now since her eldest son's death, but she frequently let it be known that she missed him like it had been yesterday. Every time she mentioned him, guilt laced through Valentine.

"Of course he would have, Mother," Jemima said gently, placing a hand on her sleeve. "But we are happy to accompany you tonight."

"Accompany *me*?" their mother responded with a sniff. "We are going so that the two of you can spend time with your peers. We must ensure our respectability among this set, my dears, and both of you *will* do your utmost to find partners who will help raise our status and make others forget our past."

"I'm a duke, Mother," Valentine said dryly. "What does status matter?"

"It just... it just... it matters," she finally finished, and Valentine wondered whether she was going to stamp her foot to emphasize her point, so adamant she seemed. "I don't want those women looking down on me as though I am less than worthy."

"You could never be less worthy than anyone else, Mother," Valentine said gently. "Title or not."

"I am the mother of a duke," she said, pointing a finger at him. "And I deserve to be treated as such."

"Very well," Valentine said wearily as they entered the carriage, unwilling to argue with her any longer. "We will show you respectability."

As he climbed into the elaborate carriage with the beautiful pair of horses in front, all Val saw were the figures that all of this was costing him. The dresses his mother and sister wore were of the finest quality and all their visits to the most popular modiste were quickly eating into the funds Valentine had earned for himself. Not for the first time, he wished that he had the ability to ask one of the previous dukes just what he was supposed to do in order to keep the dukedom in its finest order.

A noble wife would help, he knew, as they pulled up to the plain brick building, light spilling out of the six second-story round-arched windows.

"What time is it?" Val's mother fretted.

"Quarter past eleven, I'd say," Jemima said, and Mrs. St. Vincent sat up so straight that Val wondered whether the ostrich feather on her hat would go right through the carriage roof.

"Quick! Hurry!" she said, waving a hand to shuffle them out of the carriage. "The doors will be closing soon, and we *must* be sure we gain entry."

Val and Jemima exchanged another look as they followed their mother, understanding flowing between them. They would rather be anywhere but here, but they would do this for her. Their newfound status as the Duke of Wyndham and his family may have been unwelcomed by Valentine, but it had returned life to their mother following the deaths of first their brother, Mrs. St. Vincent's beloved son, followed by their father shortly thereafter.

Valentine steeled his shoulders as they walked up to the door where they presented their vouchers.

"Very good, your grace, my ladies," the doorman said as he allowed them entry.

Valentine nearly took a step back into the darkness upon their entry. Even down here on the ground floor, the foyer was filled with gowns of every color, of the chattering voices of ladies and the scents of floral, citrus, and musky perfumes and colognes intermingling.

Now all eyes turned upon them.

Val forced a smile as he led his mother and sister through the throng to deposit their cloaks and continue upstairs to the ballroom.

Jemima firmly settled herself in a chair in the corner of the room, where Val knew she would likely spend the evening studying the people present and their interactions as though they were specimens for her latest experiment.

His mother had other plans for him.

"Oh, Valentine, over there," she said, pointing across the room, clearly not concerned with the fact that she might be spotted doing so. "That is Lady Rosthern. Her daughter is of marriageable age, and I believe she has quite a large dowry. And then over there…" She droned on and on, pointing out each woman in the room who might interest Valentine and restore their fortunes while he barely paid attention to anything she said. After she had made sure to consider each and every candidate, she slipped her arm through his and instructed him to take her for a turn about the room so that they might speak to some of the women.

Val looked longingly at the door to the corridor. He would far prefer to find himself a refreshment and enter the card room instead, but he wouldn't disappoint his mother.

Not tonight. He had disappointed his parents enough in his life. His father had died believing that his second son was nothing more than a no-good fighter who lacked the wit or intelligence to do anything with his life, whose actions had destroyed their family.

He hadn't overly cared when he had known that Matthew was there to please his parents. But now all rested on his shoulders.

So he placed a smile on his face and greeted the first pretty young woman his mother introduced him to. She had pale blonde hair, blue eyes shining out of her angelic face.

But all Val could see was a woman with midnight hair and piercing hazel eyes.

He tried to make conversation as best he could, but he was distracted, his mind elsewhere. When, he wondered, would Albert Lambert have his drawings ready? Would Rebecca accompany him once more when he came to present them? Did the fact that she worked with her father mean that she was unattached? And why was he still thinking of her as Rebecca?

He was brought back to the present when his arm began to shake and he heard his mother's voice in his ear.

"Valentine," she hissed, and he turned his attention back to the conversation.

"My apologies," he said, asking the young woman to repeat herself. After requesting a later dance, which he felt was his responsibility, particularly after he had ignored her so, his mother began to pester him as they walked away.

"What is the matter with you?" she asked in a harsh whisper. "You are acting as though you've never made polite conversation in your life!"

"I cannot say I have ever been particularly skilled at it," he said apologetically, but his mother was already shaking her head.

"You know what you must do, Valentine," she said, stopping and turning so that she was standing in front of him. "You must find a wife who will be able to raise our esteem among the *ton* and provide us the funds to support our family until you can sort out this dukedom. I know you have it in you to do what needs to be done."

Her face and voice softened.

"Your father would be proud of you were he alive, Valentine," she said, cutting through deeply to what she knew would most affect him. "You are proving yourself to be an excellent duke. Just do this one thing, Valentine. It's all I ask."

Then she assumed the persona of the elegant titled woman once more and continued on, Valentine following in her wake with an ache in his gut that had nothing to do with his earlier brandy.

* * *

"The Duke of W— was finally seen last night at Almack's, making the rounds in his search of a wife," Rebecca read aloud. "Judging by his conversations and dances with Lady A—, Lady P—, and Lady R—, one can assume he is looking for a bride who will bring a fortune with her into the marriage."

She threw the paper back down upon the table. "Disgusting. He is practically selling himself."

"Which means we will be paid," her father said with a grin as he finished his plate of eggs and toast. Rebecca pushed aside her own meal, no longer hungry.

"I thought you'd be pleased," her father said, quite lucid this morning. "You're always going on about how the most important thing is that we look after our finances."

"Yes, but this seems wrong."

"It's what they do, Becca. You know that."

Rebecca knew very well who he meant by *they* — the aristocracy. The very people who they relied on to continue their work.

"Anyway, I'd best take a look at the drawings this morning."

"I spent most of yesterday on them," Rebecca said. She and her father had developed a good working relationship. When he had moments of genius, he would add to her work or draw an idea that had been swirling in his mind. Their roles had gradually switched over the years. No longer was she the apprentice, learning from him. She now spent most of her free hours teaching herself the latest styles and modernizations. They visited every new building, taking careful stock of each new design and what was in high demand.

But Rebecca went a step further. The key to designing was to determine just how the space would be used, how the family would live in it. It was more than simply impressing the guests that came to the door.

Of course, no one could ever know that she was the primary architect, for if they did, she and her father would never work again.

They now entered their study, which looked nothing like the traditional study found in most homes.

Their two desks in the room looked like typical writing desks — until their work began. Then they would raise the top of each desk so that it was slanted on an angle, and the chair they sat on in front of it would rise and fall as they wished when they pulled a simple lever.

Rebecca led her father over to her own desk, and the two of them poured over the plans. Rebecca left her father to his musings while she took a seat at his desk and pulled out much more tedious yet required work — the ledger book.

The numbers were still written in red, causing a panicky flutter to fill her chest. If only her father hadn't seen the need to distinguish himself with the latest London neighborhood. If only he had taken a much more cautious approach, building for clients and not on speculation. If only he hadn't begun to lose his faculties during the project. If only she had seen the issues earlier and taken a greater role in it all.

If only, if only, if only.

It seemed to be all her life consisted of at the moment.

They had to sell these houses. They were sitting there, empty, taunting her. In fact, Rebecca refused to even walk by the redeveloped Mayfair street because they reminded her of what had caused their near-ruin.

She had to hope that the duke — or his mother — wouldn't find about their recent failure. He was obviously looking to make a mark for himself in his world, and hiring a failing architect would do nothing to further that.

The duke. Valentine, his mother had continued to call him. An interesting name, and a fitting one. She was sure he had broken many hearts in his day.

Rebecca must ensure that her own heart would not be one of them. She had no time for romance, particularly one that was ill fated from the start. Too much was at stake. She couldn't allow him in close as she held too many secrets close to her chest. It was not as though there was any lasting relationship available to them. Any thought that he would even consider such a thing was fanciful.

He was already out looking for a bride — as all of London now knew thanks to the gossip columns of the papers — and she was a charlatan commoner who did not have a title nor a fortune to tempt him with, but rather debt of her own.

There was only one thing to do.

Keep her distance and her head free of any thoughts of the fascinating promise of a handsome duke.

CHAPTER 5

*T*wo weeks.

It had been fourteen days since Valentine had last seen the woman who had captured his attention.

It was ridiculous that he couldn't rid her from his thoughts. He had met dozens of other women throughout those days, at the many events that his mother had dragged them to night after night. The opera, the theatre, and numerous balls and parties. He couldn't remember the last time he had an evening alone to breathe.

His traitorous sister had feigned illness the last few nights, though Valentine knew she had been busy in the ball-room she used as her laboratory.

But today was the day. The day when Albert Lambert would return with initial plans for Wyndham House.

Valentine could only hope that he would bring his daughter with him.

This time he would not be late for their meeting. In fact, he was already in the drawing room waiting with antic-ipation.

"I don't believe we should be hosting an architect in the

drawing room," his mother opined when he strode into the room, but on this he overruled her.

"The man is one of the greatest architects throughout all of England. Evidence of his work will live forever, Mother. I will not relegate him to the parlor."

"Oh, very well," she said with a huff.

"Mr. Lambert and Miss Lambert," Dexter announced, and Val shot to his feet. So she had come.

Valentine sought out her gaze but she averted it, instead greeting his mother and then taking a seat on one of the two sofas in the room.

"Well," she said. "My father is pleased to show you his ideas for your home." Finally, she looked up at him, but there was nothing upon her face but professional courtesy.

Why her father didn't speak for himself, Val wasn't sure, but he assumed it was one of his eccentricities or egoisms.

Rebecca unrolled the large scrolls on the table, moving around it as she did so. Her light blue skirts brushed against him when she walked by, and just that slight whisper of muslin over his pant leg stirred something deep within him.

"Valentine?" his mother said, digging an elbow into his side.

"Ouch," he muttered. "Yes, Mother?"

"What do you think of Mr. Lambert's designs?" Before he had a chance to begin, however, she began to recount her own thoughts on all of it. "I think it is an excellent starting point," she said. "I do enjoy the many different aspects you have drawn, and I can see how some of it would be very convenient. But I do hope you have additional ideas for something much more... oh, I don't know... *grand* and *impressive*."

"You do not like my design?" Mr. Lambert asked, his defenses raised, and Valentine cringed.

"I think, Mr. Lambert, what my mother is trying to say is

that she is looking forward to some additional embellishments to come nearer the end of the project."

At a time when he could hopefully afford them, he thought, though he didn't say it aloud.

"Er, yes," his mother said when he directed a pointed look her way.

Valentine took a closer look, ensuring that this time he was actually concentrating on what was in front of him.

He was impressed.

"Smart," he said, looking at the way the corridors flowed, where they had situated the kitchen and some of the servants' rooms. They had obviously worked from the initial plans, which he appreciated as it would keep the costs down, but they had added some of their own flair and modernizations.

"This," Rebecca said, tracing a line with her finger, "is how my father envisions installing a shower-bath. And this," she pointed beside, though it was all he could do to keep focus as he stared at that long slim finger, "is where we would put the water closet with a system that would dispense with the need for a chamber pot."

Valentine thought she was likely the only female he had ever met, besides his sister, who could speak of such things without embarrassment. It was endearing... in a strange way.

He knew others may not agree with him, but perhaps he had become rather too used to Jemima's frankness.

"The interiors may seem simplistic," she said, "but they will stand up over time. Your descendants will be able to design the interior according to the style of the day without having to undertake a great deal of structural change. Outside, my father thought to use stucco to accent the brick and pillars of iron to imitate the look of stone."

"That's ingenious," he said, impressed, and she smiled

proudly for a moment before returning to her stoic expression and nodding to her father.

"Thank you," she said simply. "Oh, and one more thing that your sister will be interested in."

"Yes?"

"Here is your conservatory," she said, pointing once more. "Its dimensions remain unchanged. We still suggest growing greenery. However, I would see if your sister has any preference for what is planted. My father has converted this back area into a laboratory. There are two tables that will extend along the back wall, with a desk to the side. Here, he would suggest hanging a wall of slate, so that she can use chalk to write and erase as needed."

"I *love* that!"

"Jemima!" their mother admonished as Valentine's sister walked through the door. Apparently, she had torn herself away long enough to listen to what ideas the architects may have. "There is no need for you to be skulking around doors," their mother continued. "Do come in and sit like the lady that you now are."

"I didn't want to bother anyone, nor stay long," Jemima said, though she took her mother's invitation and walked into the room. Val smiled slightly. He knew the real reason why she hadn't entered — she had no desire to have to stay for the entirety of the meeting in case an idea came to her and she wanted to leave. Eavesdropping meant she could stay for what she wanted to hear and then when she was bored, she could return to her work.

She leaned over the table now, looking up at Rebecca with an eager smile on her face.

"Thank you," she said earnestly, and Rebecca began to answer but then turned to her father.

"It is my father's work," she said graciously. "I simply present his ideas."

"Well, this is a good one," Jemima said.

"I cannot say I enjoy the idea of the conservatory becoming a laboratory," Mrs. St. Vincent said with a sniff, "but at the very least it is far better than having it within the ballroom."

She turned now to Valentine, her face aglow.

"Oh, Valentine, once the renovations are complete, we will hold the finest ball in all of London! It will show all that we are worthy of the title after all."

Valentine caught Rebecca's curious look at his mother's words, but she seemed to dismiss it for she returned to her father's drawings and her explanations.

Valentine couldn't keep his gaze off of her as she spoke. She came alive when she discussed the potential for the many niches of the walls, the arched doorways, her father's ideas for incorporating the Palladian aspects of the current house with the neoclassical style that he was known for.

Her cheeks were flushed, her eyes bright, her movements passionate.

Suddenly Valentine was no longer thinking about his home.

He was so distracted that when he realized all were staring at him, he knew they must have asked him for his opinion some time beforehand.

"My apologies, what was that?"

"My, you are inattentive as of late," his mother muttered, but then with the remembrance that they were not alone, she added, "though you have been so preoccupied with your new duties."

"Yes," he said, clearing his throat. "Well, one thing I can say with confidence, Mr. Lambert, is that we have certainly found the right man for the job."

"I agree," his mother said. "It has all the convenience that

Valentine desires and with a few modifications will also have the opulence that I know will impress."

The mention of such opulence gave Valentine pause, for he could be paying for these renovations at Wyndham House — not to mention Stonehall Estate — for years to come. He ran a hand over his face as he thought of the debt.

Miss Lambert obviously misread his expression for she quickly rolled up the papers and stood.

"Perhaps we should go for a tour and explain some of the various aspects of what we're proposing?"

She looked to each of them in question as she made her suggestion, and they all nodded.

They began in the ballroom, before walking in a circle to the front foyer, then to the drawing room. Miss Lambert painted a picture with her words, bringing her father's visions to life. She spoke with vivid expressions, gesticulating arms, and a wide smile. Her father commented now and again, but Valentine understood now why Lambert had his daughter work for him. Her enthusiasm was infectious.

"Sea-green walls?" Valentine's mother questioned. "I'm not sure how I feel about that. Marble busts over the fireplace? Of whom?"

"For the mansion of a duke, ancient Greek carvings," Mr. Lambert said, chiming in. "I can suggest where would be best to find them at auction."

Mrs. St. Vincent made a face.

"I'm not a particular fan of the Greek design."

"Not a fan?" Mr. Lambert responded as though she had personally insulted him. "Why, it is *because* of the Greeks that we have the very style we have today!"

Valentine noted Rebecca's deep sigh as her father began to lecture them on Greek architectural history. His mother was not at all impressed and had plenty of rebuttals to his points.

Valentine leaned in toward Rebecca.

"Shall we continue on?" he murmured.

She looked back at her father, hesitation on her face.

"I'm not sure…"

"I promise, we will not even be out of hearing. You can shout if we find ourselves undressed in close circumstances once more."

Her cheeks turned crimson.

"Your grace, I—"

"I'm teasing," he said with a laugh, realizing it had been some time since he had found such humor in anything. "But I am quite curious as to what your father has planned for the library. Perhaps you can explain it to me."

"I can," she agreed and he held out his arm to her as the two of them continued down the corridor.

"You know, it took me weeks to determine where I was going through this monstrosity of a maze that is supposedly a house," he said, turning to look at her. "You seemed to have no problem whatsoever."

"It is one of my few skills," she said with a demure smile. "I've spent my life following my father from one commission to the next. It has been rare when we found ourselves residing in our own home, as a matter of fact. Learning a new design comes fairly naturally."

"You also seem to have a great understanding of his work," Valentine remarked, and when her step faltered slightly he turned to see if there was something she had tripped on.

"I enjoy helping him," she said as they walked into the room that rose two stories, stretching out far to each side, filled with near-empty, mismatched bookshelves. "Do you enjoy reading?" she asked him, stepping away from his arm and looking up at him.

He cringed. "I am not exactly one for scholarly pursuits."

"No? Then what do you enjoy?"

He paused for a moment, considering what exactly to tell her.

"I enjoy athletic endeavors," he finally settled upon. "I, ah, didn't come by my title following a conventional path so my time as a youth was occupied by other pursuits."

"I see," she murmured, her curiosity evident, but she was polite enough not to ask questions. He supposed years among the residences of the nobility had taught her that.

"Well, if there are certain sports you enjoy, I'm sure my father would be interested in knowing more about them. He could perhaps incorporate them into the building plans or the green."

"The green?" His stomach dropped. He hadn't planned for any landscaping.

"Yes," she said, her brow furrowing. "Unless you wouldn't like us to include it? I just thought it would be a pity, what with your land encompassing most of the neighborhood's greenery."

Of course his mother would want all to see their greens as some of the finest in London.

He sighed.

"Very well, include the green."

"Right. Well, if there is anything you would like changed, do let us know."

He nodded.

"Now," he said, looking around him, "about this library."

"Yes," she said, her smile widening. "Close your eyes for a moment and I'll describe it for you."

She closed her own and began speaking. Valentine chose not to do as she said, but instead watched her.

Light from the tall library windows filtered in and high-lighted her prominent cheekbones as she tilted her head back and begin to describe the large French windows that her father had designed to lead out of the library and onto a balcony that would overlook the gardens beyond.

"We cannot always be out in nature, but we can bring nature into us," she said, opening her eyes, looking at him now with rapture. "Across from the windows will be a mirror so that the outdoors shines throughout the room. Everywhere you walk you will have a view of the trees beyond. With the doors open, the fresh scents will waft through the air. The columns around the library, which are not yet completed, as well as the bookshelves will be created out of rough-hewn wood that will capture the essence of the trees beyond it, bringing them indoors. Oh, your grace," she said, opening her eyes, "it will be utterly beautiful."

Valentine was speechless. He was entranced — not by her words, nor her father's designs.

But by her.

CHAPTER 6

$\mathcal{R}$ebecca stared at her wardrobe, unsure of what to pack.

After their meeting with the Duke of Wyndham, he had been hesitant about embarking upon their renovations until he knew what would be required at his country estate. His mother encouraged them to go ahead and begin in London, but Rebecca admired his foresight.

She admired a great many other things about him as well, but that was neither here nor there.

So now they were all about to take a six-hour carriage ride to visit Stonehall Estate, where they would view the manor and provide plans for it as well. This would be a bit more difficult, however, for as expansive as the estate was, they would be staying and dining with the family. It would be much more difficult to cover her father's absent-mindedness there. At least she could blame most of it on the eccentricities of an artist.

One never knew, however, when he would say something that would prove to be their undoing.

What she did pack in her valise was the ledger book as

well as the current finances for the development, the Atticus Project, that her father had built and subsequently failed to sell. What should have been one of his greatest legacies was ruining them.

She reached behind her to try to massage her shoulders. She carried tightness in the muscles when she became tense — as she was right now and would be at least until they returned home once more.

Perhaps the duke and his family would leave them be, relegating them to mere servant status. While it was somewhat insulting and her father would grow incensed if he was ever treated in such a way, at the same time it would keep the St. Vincents from learning the truth.

This had better be a quick visit.

Rebecca also didn't want to admit how much she was looking forward to spending time with the duke. After being among noblemen for so much of her life, she had thought she had known what to expect when she met him. She had been mistaken.

He was frank and forthright. He spoke with directness and a tone that was not common among the noble set.

Rebecca consulted old issues of the gossip columns — a page she had typically overlooked, until quite recently when every morning she ran to the paper and eagerly flipped through until she found it, to learn more of who the Duke of W— had been seen with. She had learned that he had not come from noble beginnings at all. It was all quite a mystery, but as far as the newspaper reported, he was a commoner who had learned he was named heir to the previous Duke of Wyndham. It noted his brother had died and his cousin had been deemed illegitimate, but nothing further. He had gone from a middle-class man with a profession — though what profession, the paper didn't say — to duke in less time than one could open a door.

As she had to right now. The Duke of Wyndham and his family would be here at any moment, and she didn't want her father greeting them. He was liable to tell them that he didn't want any salesmen at his door and they should go away.

Rebecca worried her bottom lip as she watched out the window. Her father insisted that he would ride alongside the carriage like a proper gentleman. She had tried to convince him that it would be perfectly acceptable for him to ride inside the carriage with the women, but he had refused.

As it was, Rebecca thought it was rather strange that the family had offered the architect to accompany them for the journey, but then, the St. Vincents did not seem to be the typical noble family.

Which was evidenced by the overly cheerful greeting she received less than an hour later, when she entered the carriage.

"Miss Lambert!" Miss St. Vincent exclaimed, holding her hand out. "How wonderful that you are joining us."

"Yes, it is lovely to see you, Miss Lambert," Mrs. St. Vincent said from beside her daughter with a slight sniff. "I didn't know that we were to expect you to accompany us."

"My father is more efficient in his work when I am with him," Rebecca said, telling the truth. "I hope you don't mind."

"Not at all," Miss St. Vincent said with a smile of welcome. "It's only a few hours' journey to Stonehall Estate — just the perfect amount of time for us to come to know one another better. Please, call me Jemima. Everyone does."

Rebecca could sense the sincerity in her words and settled in across from her.

"Then I am Rebecca."

Despite spending the journey continually looking out the window to ensure that her father still followed the carriage and concerning herself about just what he was saying to the Duke of Wyndham, Rebecca enjoyed herself. Jemima was lovely company and asked one question after another about Rebecca's father's work until finally, Rebecca had the opportunity to ask her a question of her own.

"Before the duke became... the duke, where did you live?" she asked, always curious to learn more of previous residences of clients to gain insight.

She sensed Mrs. St. Vincent stiffen, but Jemima softly smiled.

"In a pleasant middle-class home in Hungerford," she said, "far from London and our Mayfair mansion, though quite close to our estate. We were from the same area, as distant family of the previous duke."

"Truly?" Rebecca said.

"Yes," Jemima said with a nod. "Valentine's inheritance of the dukedom was rather... unexpected, you could say."

"Are not all of these lineages quite detailed?" Rebecca couldn't help but ask, intrigued.

"Typically," Jemima agreed. "However, in this case, we had always thought that our cousin was to inherit. Then he was deemed illegitimate and the College of Arms had to discover who was next in line. It came down to Valentine or another cousin, and eventually, Val was declared the duke."

"He must have been pleased," Rebecca said politely, but Jemima laughed.

"Hardly."

"Jemima!" Mrs. St. Vincent finally spoke, but Jemima shrugged one of her delicate shoulders.

"It's the truth, Mama," she said. "And I hardly think that Rebecca will judge us as many of the *ton* would."

"Of course not," Rebecca said demurely. "Did the duke have a profession?" she asked, but before Jemima could say anything, Mrs. St. Vincent leaned forward and placed a hand on her daughter's knee.

"I must call for the coach to stop," she said. "I am feeling a trifle ill."

"Very well, Mama," Jemima said, calling to the driver to stop for a moment.

Rebecca was no simpleton. Mrs. St. Vincent clearly wasn't pleased with her daughter sharing the family secrets, as evidenced by the fact that she took Jemima aside once they stopped and was obviously firmly chastising her.

Rebecca took the moment to check on her father.

"How is your ride?" she asked when he reined in next to her.

"Just fine," he said. "I am, in fact, inspired by the views."

"Good," she said, relieved.

"Now, when will we arrive at the viscount's manor?"

"The duke's, Father."

"The Viscount of Alberta," he said, frowning. "We have had this commission for months now, Becca. Are you not looking forward to seeing his children again?"

Rebecca's heart sank. Her father had designed and over-seen the building of Lord Alberta's estate over a decade ago.

"Father," she said gently, placing a hand on his knee so that he would look at her. "We are going to the Duke of Wyndham's, do you not remember?"

"Of course," he said brusquely. "Now, when we get there, bring me the plans for the London development, will you?"

As he clicked at his horse and rode over to the duke, Rebecca rubbed her shoulder where the tension had begun again. She could only hope that her father would speak of things that wouldn't capture the duke's attention.

"I'm sorry."

Rebecca turned swiftly to find Jemima at her shoulder. "My mother is not entirely comfortable with speaking of our past. We come from a much different place, and others do judge us for it."

"I understand," Rebecca said softly so that Mrs. St. Vincent couldn't hear their conversation. "Our lives have been interesting as well, being commoners and yet spending so much time among the nobility. I apologize for my questions."

"My mother… she has known loss as well," Jemima said, her smile faltering for a moment, but she didn't further elaborate. "Now all she can think of is holding on to what, to her, was a miracle."

"The dukedom."

"Yes." Jemima nodded sagely, her expression indecipherable, as she gazed off into the distance. "It seems she is prepared to continue on. We are not far now."

Rebecca nodded, seeking out her father once more as they returned. Instead of capturing his attention, however, her gaze arrested on the duke. He made a fine figure on his mount, that was for certain. The sun cast a bronze light on his chiseled jaw, a gust of the wind that marred the otherwise fine day pushing back a sandy lock of hair from his forehead — a lock that Rebecca would very much like to be teasing with her fingers herself.

Ridiculous, she told herself as his eyes caught hers, and one side of his lips curled in recognition of her study of him. Her breath caught, but she mercifully managed a brief nod, hoping that he would suppose she was simply admiring the scenery when he had entered her vision.

Not likely, but one could hope.

She turned quickly and re-entered the carriage, where Rebecca thought it prudent to change the topic of conversation, judging by the way Mrs. St. Vincent was avoiding her gaze, her hands in her lap gripping one another tightly as she stared out the window as though the scenery proved far more interesting.

"Tell me of Stonehall Estate," Rebecca said imploringly. "Have you been before? What is it like?"

"It's finished, at least," Mrs. St. Vincent said, and Rebecca nodded, waiting for more. When the elder St. Vincent woman said nothing, Jemima took up the conversation.

"It is most impressive," she said, "though it was built some time ago — in the 1500s, I believe. It is built of fine materials and structurally, it is sound."

Apparently, Jemima was not particularly keen on aesthetics.

"Well, we look forward to touring it — both of us."

"We can hardly wait for you to see it," Mrs. St. Vincent said dryly.

When Jemima turned to her with a secret smile, Rebecca knew the two of them would be fast friends.

CHAPTER 7

*V*alentine's saving grace was that he hadn't had to spend the entirety of the six-hour ride to Stonehall Estate ensconced in a carriage with Rebecca Lambert.

He would hardly have been able to contain himself.

As it was, he was tempted to rush over and escort her down from the carriage as though he was courting the woman. Thankfully, his mother was sure to provide her arm for him to assist her.

Had he remained simply Valentine St. Vincent and not become the Duke of Wyndham, Rebecca would have made a suitable bride for him. In fact, she likely would have been above him on the social ladder, as it were.

How quickly things could change.

He watched her now as she surveyed the exterior of the estate. *His* estate. How the man who had hardly a house to call his own was now holding an extravagant mansion in London and a countryside estate that could fit his family ten times over, not to mention the various other holdings he now owned, was still beyond him.

Not just beyond him… but overwhelming him. He was

drowning in these estates, which he could barely find his way around much less find his way out the other side of the debt that had latched onto his coattails and was dragging it off of him.

Valentine heard some mutterings coming from behind him, and he turned to see that Mr. Lambert had also dismounted and was speaking to himself as he climbed the front steps. The man had actually proven to be an entertaining companion throughout the ride here. He spoke of various works he had completed in the past and was quite candid in describing many of the families he had worked with and for. Val had learned quite a few lessons in architecture in the short few hours — everything from how to blend styles when adding onto a structure, as he had designed an additional wing at Remingford Hall, to how Mr. Lambert had added a staircase outside of a house leading up to an earl's bedroom so that his mistresses could easily enter and exit without his wife being aware of their presence.

Now, however, the architect did not seem pleased.

"This is not at all how I remember it," he was saying, waving his hands in the air as he looked up at Stonehall. "Not at all."

"Have you been here before, Mr. Lambert?" Val asked, surprised. Surely Mr. Lambert would have mentioned knowing the old duke.

"I think he means how he had pictured it before arriving." Miss Lambert's voice from behind him was like a cool, clear river washing over him. Her words were practiced, unhurried, though he sensed some kind of apprehension in her eyes as she lifted her skirts and climbed the stairs.

"I see," Valentine said, though he didn't, really. But who was he to argue with the methods and opinions of one of the most highly regarded architects in all of England? "I shall

48

have the housekeeper and butler show you to your rooms," he said, "then we can begin a tour."

"Very well," Rebecca said, smiling politely at him. "We look forward to it."

He would have looked forward to a moment alone with her, but then, one never received all he wished for.

Just the things he didn't — like a dukedom.

* * *

JEMIMA'S DESCRIPTION of Stonehall Estate had been practical, measured, and factual.

She had left out many of the pieces that made it so intriguing.

Such as the way the gold leaf and pale yellow stone glistened in the afternoon sun. The intricate detailing, the Belvedere turrets, the wide expanse of lush yet slightly overgrown and tangled garden. Rebecca had heard of Stonehall Estate before, of course, but she couldn't have been prepared for just how beautiful it was to behold.

Then there was its current owner.

"Miss Lambert."

Of course, the duke would be the only one present in the foyer when she arrived for the beginning of the tour after settling in their rooms. Wasn't that just the way of it?

"What do you think of Stonehall Estate so far?"

"It's magnificent," she said truthfully, and he laughed.

"I was overwhelmed by it when we first visited," he said, clasping his hands behind his back as he looked down at her, his arms straining his jacket. He cut a fine figure in his navy waistcoat, fawn trousers, and starched cravat, but Rebecca had the impression that he was not particularly comfortable in such attire. "The great hall alone is larger than the house I was born in. I needed a map to find my bedchamber."

"How many estates did you inherit?" she asked.

"Six in all," he said, looking around him, and Rebecca sensed some desperation on his part. "The others seem to be in much better shape, however, though they are all fairly stripped of their finer decor, as you will soon see here."

"I'm sorry to hear it," Rebecca murmured. He was in quite the conundrum, it seemed, but she wasn't quite sure how to help him. It wasn't as though she was a wealthy heiress, and they certainly couldn't work without compensation.

"Valentine, Miss Lambert." Mrs. St. Vincent practically sailed into the room once more. "My apologies on my tardiness. I had forgotten how exhausting it can be to climb the stairs to the second floor. *This* is why I typically remain in London."

"You did not need to accompany us, Mother."

"Oh, but I did. This drafty ruin needs much work, and I have many ideas that I am quite keen on sharing with Mr. Lambert. Where *is* Mr. Lambert?"

Rebecca had been wondering that herself.

"Perhaps I best go check on him."

"He could be wandering the place himself again," the duke said, and Rebecca stilled.

"As I found him in the London house," he explained, and Rebecca nodded slowly. Thank heaven the duke seemed to be under the impression that her father simply had creative tendencies. They must keep this stay as short as possible so that he did not realize anything further. Not only would they lose this project, but if others assumed her father to have gone mad…

"Where is Jemima?" she asked Mrs. St. Vincent, who waved a hand in the air.

"Oh, she has already holed herself up somewhere. She said she would see us for dinner. Really," she huffed, "I don't understand the girl, but so be it."

"We should save this tour for later," the duke said, but Rebecca was eager to begin working on the plans. The sooner she could finish the work, the sooner they could leave and none would be the wiser of how they managed.

She could also then escape the duke and her inexplicable longings for him. She was usually much more reasonable than this. The duke was terribly striking, that was certain — but she knew better than to let a handsome face turn her head.

It was more than that, however. It was the fact that he didn't act like a nobleman, that she could sense a vulnerability lurking in the depths of his tough exterior. And that she thought — she hoped — he had some desire for her in return.

"This estate is a beautiful monstrosity."

They turned in unison as Rebecca's father strode into the room. She cringed at his forwardness — but then, this was the same man who had become famed through England for his work and was not humble about it. He was just being himself.

"I am not sure what you mean," Mrs. St. Vincent said with icy politeness.

"The baroque is beautiful, and the south domed front is one of the most captivating I have ever seen," he explained. "But this building is the work of such a variety of men and styles that it will be difficult to ever meld it into one grand estate. Pieces of it are beautiful, but together..." He shook his head with such melancholy one would have thought a loved one had been declared too ill to continue on. "I am unsure as to whether or not I can work on such a building."

Rebecca held her breath, waiting to see if the duke would be insulted. Thankfully, he gave a low chuckle instead.

"I understand, Mr. Lambert," he said. "Why do we not

walk around the house, and you can provide any expertise? If you decide it is out of your depth then... so be it."

They began the long walk around the house, missing most of the bedchambers as there would be no work required of them there, at least at this time. The duke led the tour, though Mrs. St. Vincent had many grand ideas — most, she admitted to having seen in the homes of others within the nobility, and she had no grasp of style or continuity. Rebecca chose not to comment. Though her father had just as many suggestions as Mrs. St. Vincent, all of those Rebecca recognized as elements he had included in his previous work.

"The estate is beautiful, to be sure," Rebecca commented. "The gardens, the courtyard, the impressive staircase. But it is so... empty."

"Yes," the duke agreed. "Many of the paintings and sculptures were sold by the previous duke. Some remain — the family portraits, of course — but it is quite unfortunate."

"We will purchase them back," Mrs. St. Vincent said determinately, though Rebecca didn't miss the pained expression on the duke's face and she could tell that Mrs. St. Vincent would not appreciate Rebecca's questions.

"What is needed," Rebecca's father finally said, "is an addition. Something which will allow you to leave a legacy and tie in the remainder of the styles throughout the house."

"An addition?" the duke's lips strained and his brow furrowed. "That would be costly, would it not?"

"Nothing is too costly," his mother said, sweeping her hand about. "For now that you are duke, my dear, we will soon have everything set to rights, will we not?"

The duke didn't reply, though his expression said he clearly didn't completely agree with his mother.

"Why do we not reconvene this evening at dinner?" the

duke asked as they returned to the foyer. "We can discuss much more then."

"Very well," Mrs. St. Vincent said with a sigh. "I, for one, am exhausted."

Fanning herself, she swooped away, while Rebecca's father had already left, muttering to himself about Elizabethan and baroque, of degrading it and dispensing with beauty.

"Would it be possible for my father and I to use a library or another room for a study of sorts while we are here?" she asked the duke now, somewhat awkward to find herself alone in his presence once more.

"Of course," he agreed, standing and holding his arm out. "Perhaps the long gallery, I believe it has been called. I'll have the butler fetch you all that you might need."

"Thank you," she said, smiling at him in return, wishing that she had the quick wit and social breeding to know how to make pleasant conversation with him, but alas, all that currently came to her mind was assessing this estate that had become his so very recently.

"Your grace..." she began, unsure exactly of how to put her thoughts into words without insulting him.

"Yes?"

"It seems to me that the dukedom is... well, it's impoverished."

"You would be correct," he said with a crooked smile.

"I question, then, why hire my father? Why take up these renovations at this time?"

He nodded, but instead of answering her, he asked another question instead. "Why would you question me so, when this will be a significant commission for your father?"

It was a good question, and one that Rebecca asked herself. She supposed she simply didn't have it within her to bring another to ruin in order to further their own finances.

But as he chose not to answer her question, she evaded his as well.

"This is a beautiful estate," she said, holding her hand up as she circled the grand hall they were now walking through. "It could use some restoration, but perhaps nothing too extravagant, though I do agree that your London home must be seen through to completion. You could, however, simply live in this for now, until the time comes when you find yourself more… able to continue forward."

"Perhaps you are right," he said with a shrug. "But a legacy must be made, Miss Lambert."

He said the words so sarcastically, she knew it was not him who desired such a thing.

"I understand this is important to your mother," she said slowly. "But you are the duke, are you not?"

"I am," he agreed but then hesitated. "My mother and father... they never expected me to amount to much. Then my brother died, and suddenly it was up to me to look after the family, although it has not been easy. I have been nothing but a disappointment." A wistful sigh slipped out, though Rebecca wondered if he was even aware of it. "I must change that."

"Very well," she said as they came to the door of the gallery. She longed to ask him more questions, to better understand his story and who he was, but she sensed that if she pushed, she would lose any of his trust and would never learn more again. "I should begin my notes for my father, then."

"I'll call the butler."

Yet despite their words, they both stood there staring at one another for a moment, neither seeming to want to leave.

Finally the duke nodded, turned, and walked away.

CHAPTER 8

*V*alentine's head pounded something fierce as he stared at the ledgers in front of him.

It was difficult to concentrate with all of his swirling thoughts. Rebecca and her father were entrenched in the long gallery just down the corridor. He had heard their murmured voices when he walked by not long before. How nice it must be to have an assistant, someone to work with and lean on.

Rebecca's melodic voice had wafted down the hall and into his head. Once it filled him, it was hard to forget it. He could picture as she had looked this afternoon, when he had found it difficult to keep from touching her as often as he could. She had been encased in a crimson dress that was quite becoming on her, suiting her dark features and accentuating her bold hazel eyes with the dark lashes that dipped so low when she looked to the ground, as she often seemed to do around him.

He had the impression that, for some reason, she wanted to be out of his presence, though why, he had no idea.

Unless... unless she was fighting the same attraction as he? The idea both excited and terrified him.

Valentine pushed the thought aside and returned to the ledgers. He had never been particularly proficient in mathematics, nor many of the subjects he took in school as a young boy. Eventually, he and his father had decided to stop fighting about it all and he had left school and chased other pursuits which were not only lucrative but that he actually enjoyed — until they became a detriment to them all.

Matthew had been the one to follow in his father's footsteps, studying to become a physician. It was Matthew who'd been going to help the world, look after their family, and be the son his parents had longed for. Then Matthew had been killed, and it was entirely Valentine's fault.

Val ran a hand over his face. Thank goodness he had Jemima. Although his sister, with her own brilliance, was often a reminder of all that he lacked.

He thought of Rebecca and her father entrenched in the long gallery. That was what he needed — help. Someone who understood all of this much better than he.

"Howard!" he called to his butler, who appeared in moments. The man seemed to lurk the halls, awaiting his summons.

"Yes, your grace?"

"The steward that was here before I arrived..."

"The one you were rid of, your grace?"

"The very one," Val replied. As soon as he had realized the ledgers hadn't been updated in years, he had been rid of the man. "Did you know much about him?"

"I, ah, do not wish to speak out of turn..."

"Please do," Val said, realizing that the one aspect he did enjoy about being a duke was the fact that people did as he bid.

"He was a lazy bastard," Howard said, then straightened and returned to his usual reserve, "your grace."

What Val needed to do more than anything else, was to find people he could trust. People who would do for him what he couldn't do for himself. The problem was determining who he could put his faith in. It was why most of those he hired had been friends or acquaintances before he became a duke. Most others, he had found in his experience thus far, all used him to further their own connections. Those who didn't latched onto him in the hopes of leeching wealth and prestige.

Valentine had a three-step plan. First, he would fight for short-term funds. Then, a wife to regain the Wyndham prestige. That, however, wouldn't be enough to save the dukedom for his heirs. For he refused to do what the old duke had done to him. Thirdly, he needed to get all of the affairs in order.

"Howard?"

"Yes, your grace?"

"Is there a local magistrate?"

"There is."

"Have him meet me here tomorrow," he said. "In the meantime, I am going to prepare a letter to be sent to my solicitors in London. We need to turn things around." He sighed. "And we need to do it now."

* * *

REBECCA LEANED back in her chair, rolling her shoulders to try to ease the tension.

She had been sitting too long hunched over, as was often the case. She picked up the plans before her and moved with them to stand in front of the fireplace before stretching out over the rug so that she could lie on her stomach and review them. Perhaps something would miraculously come to her if she changed positions.

She tapped her pencil against her forehead as the fire crackled beside her. This was a long, drafty room. At one point in time, it had been a gallery of some sort, but as the duke had noted during their initial tour, many of the paintings had disappeared. Likely they'd been sold over the years as the previous duke lay ailing in his bed.

It was sad, really. This beautiful estate, so mismanaged, not looked after to keep its prestige. And now it was all up to Valentine to regain its status.

Rebecca could sense his discomfort in taking on this new position. Most men she knew would do anything to be in his shoes. But if one wasn't prepared for such a life, she could see how it could become rather isolating and a great burden.

She returned her thoughts to her task at hand. The estate included many spectacular rooms and fantastic views, but it was as though each wing was a manor in itself. They all circled the courtyard in the center, an Elizabethan holdover. Rebecca was surprised it had lasted so long without being given over to another style more popular of the day. The courtyard could be beautiful, she knew, but at the moment each wing of the house functioned as its own separate entity, and the courtyard had been seemingly forgotten. Rebecca would have liked to have worked with the original style, but her father was insisting on redesigns to bring in the neoclassical he was known for.

The dukedom, however, did not seem to have any financial wellbeing. How the duke was going to fund all of this, Rebecca had no idea, though she supposed that needn't be her concern.

Except she couldn't, in good conscience, design extravagance such as a new wing when the duke would never recover from the debt.

She had tried to discuss all of this with her father over the past couple of days they had been here, but today had been a particularly unproductive day. He was convinced that they were at Remingford Hall, and when he did have more lucid moments he was determined that he needed to be designing the brand new wing.

"But there are rooms within the current estate that haven't even been touched in years," Rebecca had argued, remembering the dusty, musty rooms that the duke had shown them on their initial tour.

"Think of how grand it could be, Rebecca," was his response. "All who come to visit the duke will be speaking of my finest accomplishment!"

Except it wouldn't actually be *his* accomplishment, for her father hadn't been putting pencil to paper. Instead, it was Rebecca who had taken a mixture of his ideas as well as her own and created the designs, and she who would help direct the work.

She looked around her at the long, empty gallery. The estate had a library, but it was in a separate wing. A wing that, at the moment, housed nothing but guest chambers and a room that she assumed had once been a billiards room but was now lacking a billiards table.

Inspired, she began to draw, her pencil seemingly moving of its own will, removing current walls, combining rooms, and adding in various aspects. The duke enjoyed the outdoors, and she had noted his eyes light up at the idea of the French windows in his library in his London house.

Perhaps with a few additions here and there…

Rebecca didn't know how much time had passed, nor how long she had worked. When inspiration struck her, everything else around her no longer mattered, only the ideas that flowed from her heart, through her mind, to her hand and pencil onto paper.

"Miss Lambert?"

Rebecca jumped, pushing herself up to her heels, nearly falling over backward in her haste. She had no wish for the duke to find her stretched out on the floor of his gallery in the middle of the night.

"Your grace," she greeted him, lifting her hand to her head to determine what state her hair was currently in, dismayed to find that tendrils had fallen out of their pins and were now strewn around her shoulders. She must look like quite a fright.

"What are you doing?" he asked, sauntering across the room, and Rebecca took advantage of the length of the room to quickly fold and cover her drawings.

"I, ah, I must have fallen asleep," she said, with what she hoped was a convincing smile of innocence. "I was cleaning up some of the notes I took earlier while helping my father."

He nodded, causing a stab of guilt to course through Rebecca at his easy belief in her. As he walked toward her, her heart rate quickened, but then he brushed past her and began to stoke the fire, which had fallen to embers. She swallowed hard, for his large frame seemed to fill the room and make her suddenly feel quite small.

"It's late," he murmured now, turning around and leaning back against the marble that surrounded the fireplace.

"It is," she agreed, her teeth scraping over her bottom lip as she searched for something to say. He cut an imposing figure, and she knew that she shouldn't be here, alone with the duke in the gallery-turned-workroom, but at the same time, it seemed so right to be here with him that she couldn't bring herself to leave.

"We probably shouldn't be alone together," he said, reading her thoughts, to which she shook her head.

"No," she answered, her voice just above a whisper, "but here we are."

He ran a hand through his hair as he practically dropped himself into one of the upholstered green armchairs that were pushed against the wall of the room. The fire lit the chiseled planes of his face, leaving the rest of it in shadows.

"Would you like to talk about it?" she asked, and he looked up suddenly.

"About what?"

"Whatever has you so despondent," she said, taking a seat in the chair next to him, forgetting for a moment her current state of disarray

"It's nothing," he said, waving a hand in the air. "Nothing worth speaking of."

"Nothing worth speaking of, or nothing you *think* should be worth speaking of?"

He frowned. "You are talking in circles."

She chuckled under her breath.

"You were seemingly gifted a dukedom overnight," she said, resting her chin on her fist as she leaned on the arm of her chair, studying him. "Most would see that as a great boon, would think you to be a very lucky man. But your dukedom is impoverished. You are suddenly responsible for much more than simply your family. And you always thought it would be your brother looking after them."

She paused for a moment, tense, worried she had said too much. He stared at her in shocked silence for a couple of seconds before finally snorting and looking away from her.

"My sister talks far too much."

"My apologies, your grace. I simply thought that perhaps you needed someone to talk to. Someone who didn't matter."

Those blue eyes returned to her now, holding her captive in their stare. He straightened, losing some of his defeated slump.

"Please don't call me 'your grace,'" he said. "I hate it."

"Wyndham, them?"

"Valentine is fine."

"Very well… Valentine."

"And you, Miss Lambert, should not say that you do not matter. For you matter very much."

Heat rose in Rebecca's cheeks, then spread down her neck. She inwardly cursed, for she knew her skin was turning red and she was thankful for the darkness that permeated the room, lit only by the fire's glow.

"Rebecca, please," she said. "And to you, I am simply my father's secretary. You can share your thoughts with me without worry that they will go any farther or have any repercussions."

He nodded before leaning his head back and looking up at the cherubs dancing across the ceiling.

"Through all of this," she said after his continued silence, "are you all right?"

CHAPTER 9

*S*he was more than a pretty face.

There was depth to Rebecca Lambert's soul. Why she cared about him, he had no idea. Indirectly, she worked for him, that was true. But she needn't sit here and ask him questions, provide him an outlet to share, simply for what he would pay her father.

She asked him how he had fared through all of this. The truth was, no one had really asked him that. All had assumed that he had been so fortunate, to have gone from a man with nearly nothing to the Duke of Wyndham. Only Jemima had really understood, and even then, she had commiserated with him more than had any sympathy for him.

It had been a burden. One he didn't want.

But he couldn't tell Rebecca that. He was not only a man, but a duke now, and vulnerability led to weakness.

"I am fine," he said, despite the disbelief that crossed her face at his words. Tendrils of her midnight black hair had escaped from their pins and now framed her face, the slightest bit of wave providing softness to her prominent cheekbones and pointed chin.

"Truly?" she asked softly, to which he nodded.

"Of course," he said. "What man would not desire to become one of the most powerful men in England?"

"A man who enjoys other pursuits. A man who has no taste for additional responsibility," she countered, and he leaned forward in his seat, placing his elbows upon his knees as he looked up at her.

He lifted a hand and loosened his cravat, before wrenching it off of his neck entirely and placing it over the arm of his chair. "I hate those things," he muttered, looking up, expecting her to be shocked. Instead, her brows were raised and her stare seemed to see through all his pretense, as though she had already known his sentiments. "They are just so starched and damned uncomfortable, as though they are choking a man," he said in defense.

"You should try wearing stays," she said dryly, and he couldn't help himself.

He laughed. "You are refreshing, Rebecca, do you know that?" he said, interlocking his fingers and lifting them behind his head. "I have been around the *ton* for too long now. I had forgotten what it is like to speak to someone who understands."

"Someone common."

"Someone honest. Someone truthful."

For a moment, he wondered if he saw a flash of guilt in her eyes, but in a second it was gone once more.

"I am no saint," she murmured, and he shrugged a shoulder.

"I never said that," he responded. "I certainly am not. Far from it, in fact. The truth is, Rebecca…" he took a breath, "…I am not equipped to take on this role. I have no knowledge of what it means to be a duke. I barely finished any schooling, let alone have the learnings of how to balance books or manage agriculture or understand Parliament. The only way I know how to solve disputes is with my fists."

Finally, something seemed to unsettle her, for the corners of her mouth dipped at his declaration.

"Do you not enjoy violence, then, Rebecca?"

"I—" He could tell she wanted to attempt to lie to be polite, but she stopped herself. "Not particularly. You were a fighter, then?"

"You could say that."

It was the truth. He had been a fighter in the past. He didn't see the need to tell her that he still was.

She was silent for a moment, and his defenses rose slightly as he sensed that she might be judging him.

"Well, we all have our pasts," she said pluckily before sobering somewhat. "That doesn't mean that you cannot take on the role that has been entrusted to you."

"I have neither the skill nor the knowledge," he pointed out, but that didn't seem to deter her.

She leaned forward in her seat, which meant their knees were but inches away from one another, and he was losing himself in the forest of her bronzed green eyes.

"People can accomplish great things without necessarily possessing the skill or knowledge required," she said earnestly, and as much as he wanted to believe her, Val tilted his head at her doubtfully.

"I hardly think—"

"What matters is that you have the *drive* to succeed. That you have the will to do what it takes and that you do not doubt yourself."

She paused for a moment as though considering what else she might say. "My father... well, there are certain aspects of his work that he requires help with."

"For which you perform as his secretary?"

"Yes!" she exclaimed. "Exactly. Yet all know him as a great architect, one whose name will be remembered through history."

"I hardly think that a man hiring his daughter as a secretary is the same thing as having no fortitude whatsoever to look after one's own land and responsibilities. However, Rebecca, you need not fear, for I have already come to the same conclusion that you have suggested."

"You have?"

"I have," he nodded. "I need to find men. Men I can trust, who can look after the estates and who can help me gain a profit once more."

She narrowed her eyes at him, as though assessing him and finding him worthy. "Smart."

"Do not tell me that you approve of me, Rebecca?" he asked, lifting an eyebrow, and she laughed.

"I approve of this particular idea," she said, but then her chuckle slowly diminished. "Though a duke such as yourself hardly requires the approval of a common woman whose only accomplishment is assisting her father."

He leaned in closer to her, sensing that in doing so he slightly unsettled her.

"Somehow, Rebecca, I have the feeling that your father needs you more than you let on."

"You do?" she said, her voice slightly higher than usual.

"Yes," he said, eyeing her. "You clearly keep him grounded, focused. He's the creative type, while you, I'm sure, are the practical one in the family."

Her gaze became shuttered.

"Of course."

Somehow he had the feeling he had insulted her, though he had no idea just how he had done so, for he had only meant to remark on how well she and her father worked together.

"And then, your grace, do not forget your dowry."

"My dowry?" he repeated, confused for a moment.

"Yes, the one you will receive when you wed," she reminded him, and he felt a fool for as they had sat here conversing by the firelight, he had completely forgotten. "Perhaps your bride will also possess some knowledge on the management of an estate such as yours."

"I doubt it," he muttered.

"Why?" she implored. "Because women do not have it within them to do such work?"

"No," he said, frowning at her. "Because women are not provided the education on how to manage an estate. She would be in the dark as much as I am."

"I see," Rebecca said, showing her chagrin as she looked down at her lap once more.

"You are so eager to find fault in my words," he said, reaching out a finger, nudging it under her chin and tilting up her face to look at him. "But know, Rebecca, that I have no aim to belittle you. I know that women are capable of many great things — just look at my sister." He paused, musing for a moment, "Although, Jemima has not exactly concluded anything great yet, I have every faith that she will."

"Not many men would say such a thing," she said, her eyes wide now as they met his. "Particularly not a duke."

"Well, I am not just any duke, now am I?" he asked quirking an eyebrow.

"No," she responded, a shyly seductive smile on her face. "You most certainly are not."

Before he could think of what he was doing or the repercussions of it, he bent his head and took those lush, cherry lips with his.

She gasped in surprise, and he waited for her to lean back or to push him away, but she surprised him. She paused for a moment as though unsure of what to do, but then she began to apply the slightest bit of pressure in return.

He took that as an invitation, pressing his hand against the back of her head as he held her close against him for a moment. Her lips upon his were soft and pillowy, her hair silky smooth underneath his fingers. This was a woman who could drive him mad. She had already filled his thoughts, both awake and asleep. Now that he would have memories rather than imaginings, he didn't know how he was ever going to be free of them.

Finally, he drew back with one final quick kiss on her lips, not wanting to push her any further than she might be interested in going, nor to scare her off.

"You're quite the surprise, Rebecca," he said, still holding the back of her head near to his.

"I'm not sure that's a compliment," she said with that impish grin that so captivated him. "For it doesn't seem to me that you overly enjoy surprises."

"Usually I don't," he said, taking her slim, soft hand in his. "But for you, I will make an exception."

He bent over and kissed her hand and then, with the knowledge that if he stayed any longer she might prove altogether too much temptation, he rose and left the room.

* * *

REBECCA LISTENED to the duke's strong, firm steps echo throughout the empty long gallery as he strode away. She touched her fingertips to her lips.

She could hardly believe that her first kiss had been with the Duke of Wyndham. Not that she was going to provide him with that information. He was a duke now and as the daughter of a renowned architect, she was likely somewhat intriguing to him. Perhaps he saw her as worldly or was somehow attracted to what he thought of as a departure from who he was *supposed* to be with.

Though Rebecca wasn't stupid. She knew what she was to him. A pretty face, here in his home, available to him. Someone to, perhaps, have some fun with before he found the woman he would spend his life with — the woman who would make him respectable, who would provide him with the dowry he so desperately needed and the knowledge of this life among the nobility.

So much for her plan to avoid him.

Rebecca rose from her chair and crossed over to the plans she had folded over to hide from him. Thank goodness he hadn't seen fit to look any closer. What would he do if he found out that it was, in reality, not her father designing his London home and his estate, but her? A woman who had no formal education, but had learned all through apprenticing with her father and growing up among this life?

She had been about to admit all to him when he had kissed her, and thank goodness he had.

If she had confessed, he would then be rid of them. He might appreciate her work, but he would never allow an untried architect to oversee such important buildings.

At the worst, he, or more likely his mother, would expose her father as a fraud for all to see, despite the fact that he had, in his time, designed some beautiful, intriguing buildings.

All would be lost, and just because Rebecca had found herself falling for a man who would never be hers.

A battle was being waged within her — should she enjoy herself with the duke or allow common sense to prevail?

She closed her eyes and took a deep breath, reminding herself of what was important at the moment.

Never again, she promised herself, too rattled now to

continue any further design work as she folded her papers and placed them in the leather folio she had brought with her. If she allowed him such liberty once more, it would only increase his impression of her as a woman who was willing to participate in a brief dalliance with him.

Which was one thing she just couldn't do.

CHAPTER 10

"M r. Lambert!"

Rebecca and her father turned as one to see the duke entering the long gallery, his steps measured, a small frown on his face. "I'm eager to see what you have suggested for initial designs. Perhaps we can do a tour today?"

"A tour of Sheffield?" Rebecca's father said with a finger on his chin. "Of course."

"Not Sheffield, Mr. Lambert," the duke said, frowning, his brow furrowed as he stared at her father in confusion. "Stonehall. This estate, where we are currently residing. Which you are redesigning."

"Stonehall?" he repeated, as though he had never heard of it before. Rebecca sucked in a breath before attempting to cover for her father.

"Oh, Father," she said with a laugh that sounded forced even to herself. "You always forget the name of these estates, as many sound so alike. Of course, we would be happy to do a tour, your grace. My father still has much to do, but he would be pleased to share with you some of his initial thoughts before he delves further into his work."

"Yes, please do."

Rebecca turned to her father, praying that he would be in a sound mind.

"Sheffield Hall is one of the finest examples of Elizabethan and baroque styles meeting and working with one another," he began, and Rebecca nearly groaned aloud.

Lately, he had been speaking quite often of Sheffield Hall, at times becoming lost in the past and certain that he was in the midst of the massive renovation that he had overseen some twenty years prior when Rebecca was just a girl. She had spent much of her childhood there, for it had taken a few years to complete, so luckily she remembered it well and could usually relate back her father's musings of the estate to Stonehall. It was fortunate they had many similarities, which was likely why his former commission continued to enter his consciousness.

Rebecca turned her smile on the duke now, hoping she could distract him from her father's words.

"Perhaps later this afternoon?"

"Very well," he said with a nod, though Rebecca could tell from the bemusement on his face since her father had spoken that he was beginning to realize something was not quite right — and now she had to complete a tour of the entire house with him and her father without him learning the truth.

She placed a hand on her forehead. The sooner they could leave here the better — for more reasons than one.

* * *

VALENTINE THOUGHT that Rebecca looked nervous.

He was watching her before she noticed him. She and her

father were awaiting him in the drawing room. He had specifically *not* told his mother or sister about this particular tour. Something was off about Albert Lambert. Valentine hadn't yet determined exactly what that was, but he was determined to learn more. Perhaps a conversation when he had time alone with the man might help.

He was both pleased and disappointed in equal measure that Rebecca would be joining them. While he always welcomed her company, he would have preferred to spend more time alone with Lambert, to hear him speak himself instead of through his daughter.

It was puzzling that Rebecca spoke for him so often. One would think a famed architect such as Albert Lambert would prefer describing his work for himself. Perhaps he thought it was beneath him to do so — that others should simply appreciate his brilliance. The times he did speak of his own work, however, it was typically regarding a former commission, which could be interesting now and again, but was becoming rather tedious.

"Mr. Lambert, Miss Lambert," Valentine greeted the father and daughter as they entered the rather-dated dining room. "While I am looking forward to this tour, perhaps it would be best if it was just Mr. Lambert and me."

Rebecca's eyes widened at his words, and she looked rather frantically between him and her father.

"Oh, I'm not sure that is the best of ideas, your grace," she said quickly, her cheeks reddening. "My father welcomes the reminders that I provide him about all of the work he is doing to prepare your estate for its renovation. Though, your grace, I— he — is becoming rather concerned about what the budget is for this particular estate. Some of his ideas could be grandiose indeed, but I'm not sure—"

"Design them," Valentine said, waving a hand, "then we'll see what we can do."

73

Rebecca seemed dubious, but Mr. Lambert beamed at him in approval. Valentine was curious to see the depths of Lambert's designs.

"Let's begin here," Valentine said. "What do you see for the drawing room?"

"Oh," Rebecca said, before looking down at the pages in front of her. "What are your thoughts on covering some of these massive bare walls with tapestries, contrasting them yet complimenting them with the furnishings? I think—"

"Miss Lambert," Valentine interrupted her. "Perhaps your father could explain his vision to me."

He didn't miss the flash of anger in her eyes, but she said nothing to the contrary — how could she, when he had asked nothing particularly consequential, besides requesting that her father, the architect, explain his own drawings?

"Of course, your grace," Mr. Lambert said, though Valentine's eyes were still on Rebecca, whose shoulders were tightly clenched as she waited for her father to say more.

"I believe, your grace, that much of Stonehall should be repurposed."

"Repurposed?"

"Yes," Mr. Lambert said with a nod, beginning to walk out of the door of the room, talking as he went, waving his hands about in the air.

After a quick look at Rebecca, who seemed to have relaxed somewhat, Val followed Mr. Lambert through the room.

He continued the tour room by room, describing his vision for 'repurposing' as he explained how the family might like to utilize each room. Valentine was impressed as he always was. His plan made sense. For example, why furnish the state apartment, the most beautiful rooms of the house, for a monarch who would never visit?

The architect spoke of the many styles incorporated into

the house — its Elizabethan beginnings, the baroque elements, and of how they could celebrate its history both inside and out.

Val couldn't help but continue to steal glances at Rebecca. She was listening to her father speak with rapt attention, though he could tell she was waiting for something. Watching for something.

He, in turn, was watching her. She reminded him of forbidden fruit. Lush, sultry, with lips that were ripe for kissing.

He commanded himself to put a halt to his thoughts and refocus on Lambert.

The architect was vividly describing his vision of the estate as a whole as they left the drawing room and walked into the great room.

Lambert told of trees stretching their limbs so closely to the windows that one would think they were grown indoors. A garden with buildings nearly synonymous to those of the house itself. Accents that mimicked the very greenery that surrounded the estate.

"I can nearly see it already, Mr. Lambert," Val said with a smile of gratitude for the man. "Would you mind showing me some of the finer details of which you speak?"

"Of course," the architect said, walking over to the side wall. "We change out the current window. From this to ah…" he paused, his finger in the air as though he was waiting for the right word to come to him. "Hmm," he said, placing that finger on his chin now, scratching it. "I am actually not entirely sure what type of window we had decided, but—"

"A Venetian window, I think you had said, Father," Rebecca cut in, and the man didn't look at her, but did smile and nod.

"Of course. That is what I had told my daughter."

Valentine frowned for a moment. One would think that

an architect of Mr. Lambert's caliber would remember a certain window shape — though he supposed he had his own moments of absent-mindedness. He was just about to question Mr. Lambert when his mother swept in. So she had found them.

"Valentine!" she exclaimed as her long silk dress swirled across the room after her. "You didn't tell me you were doing a tour."

No, he most certainly had not.

"I am *so* interested in Mr. Lambert's plans," she continued on, not providing him with a moment to speak. "I can hardly *believe* you didn't tell me."

So much for his wish of a quick tour with just him and Mr. Lambert.

"Have you already gone through any of the rooms?"

"Most of the ground floor, Mother," Val replied.

"I am happy to show them to you once more," Lambert said, stepping over to Val's mother, lifting her hand to his lips, upon which he placed a quick, chaste kiss. But it had been some time since his mother had been charmed by a man, and Val could tell she was thrilled by his attention.

"Thank you, Mr. Lambert," she said as she took his proffered arm, and Val sighed. He had much to see to today, and following his mother and the architect around was not part of the list.

"I really would have liked to see the galleries," he muttered, but they were already out of earshot.

"Come, your grace," he heard in his ear, that soft, silky voice that was lighter and smoother than the finest fabric he had ever come across. "I know my father's plans well. I can show you his thoughts — they are rather inventive."

The urge to follow her was as strong as the one telling him to flee. But the more he stared at that beautiful, seductive face, the more his desire to join her, to follow her wherever she might lead him, began to win out, and finally, he nodded. Her ready smile was worth any consequences that may come.

They stepped into the long gallery, where he had found her just the night before.

"One would need some paintings in order to make this room a true gallery again, wouldn't he?" Valentine said with a quirk of a laugh, which she returned, the corners of those lips rising ever so slightly.

She had other ideas.

"Actually," she said, holding up a finger, and it was refreshing to see bare fingers for a change, rather than the gloves he had become accustomed to women of the *ton* wearing. She followed his gaze and her cheeks lightly flushed.

"Actually...?" he asked, bringing her back to the moment, for he was truly interested in what she was about to say.

"Oh, right!" her eyes gleamed as she came back to the present.

"This won't be a long gallery anymore — if you agree, that is."

"And just what would it be?" he asked, lifting an eyebrow.

"A library," she said, her lips curling into a true smile now as she spoke.

He wished he could join in her excitement, but it was difficult to do so when all he could think of was the added expense of not only designing such a room but filling it. Particularly when one added in the extension his mother wanted to complete, an entire new wing of the house.

"You don't like the idea," she said, true disappointment filling her face, surprising him. He knew she worked closely with her father, but he was surprised she would take his disinterest so personally.

"It's not that," he said, stepping toward her, taking her hands before he even realized what he was doing. "It's just...

I have few books." He smiled sheepishly. "And I'm not exactly one who cares for them. I've never been a man with a proclivity for reading."

"Ah, that's right," she said with a small smile. "The sportsman."

He rather liked that description of what he did, but he wasn't about to enter into a conversation with her about it.

"Right," was all he said, then lifted one hand from hers, grasping one of the stone shelves that was built into the wall behind her. "Books are for—"

But his words were completely cut off as the wall behind them gave way, and with a whoosh, they were both thrown into darkness — and Rebecca right into him.

CHAPTER 11

*R*ebecca went rigid.

For a moment, anyway. Then her body slowly began to melt, seemingly turning into liquid right on top of Valentine.

It was difficult to feel anything but a soft and fluid person upon Valentine. Even through their clothing, every muscle seemed to be perfectly defined underneath her. In fact, she imagined she could lie here upon him forever.

His hands rose, running down the sides and back of her body. Rebecca melted into his touch until he asked, "Are you all right? Are you hurt?" and she realized that he was simply checking for any injury.

"N-no," she stammered, as she pushed herself off of him, though her retreat was rather clumsy, so off-balance she was. "What happened? Where are we?"

"I'm not entirely sure," he said, and Rebecca heard scuffles over the floor as he stood. "Somewhere off of the long gallery?"

Rebecca pictured the plans in her mind.

ELLIE ST. CLAIR

"This explains the extra space," she murmured, and at Valentine's "hmm?" she began to explain.

"There is a space that is missing between the long gallery and the grand staircase. I thought perhaps there was something amiss with the floor plans, but perhaps the floor plans were hiding this room as much as the structure of the building itself is."

She ran a hand over the wall, the brick similar to that on the other side of it.

"This must have been built at the same time as this wing of the house," she said, more to herself than to Valentine. "It is too extensive a space to have been added at a later date."

Now that her eyes had adjusted, there was just enough light for Rebecca to see Valentine's outline before her, as well as the walls around them.

"There is a light source," she said, then stepped back, looking up to the ceiling high above them. "There must be a small cutout into the grand stairs," she said as she realized where the light was filtering in from. "Ingenious."

"It is clever," Val agreed. "But why? What would this be for?"

Rebecca began to walk along the wall, her fingers trailing the brick as she did. She stopped when her hand went into the air, no more brick apparent. She took a step forward and stubbed her toe.

"There are stairs," she said, waving Val forward, even though he likely couldn't see her well. "What do you think?" she asked, looking up at him eagerly. "Should we climb them?"

She didn't tell him just how much she yearned to do so, to learn where they would go and what she might find at the top. But this was his home, and she was a guest at the most, near a servant at the least. It was up to him.

"My curiosity is getting the better of me," he admitted.

"But I am loath to allow you up here without better light. Who knows when the last time there was a person upon these stairs."

"The light will improve the higher we get, closer to the cutout," she reassured him, letting her fingertips brush against him. "Come, let's go."

She held her hand out, willing him to take it — and was thrilled when, after the briefest moment of hesitation, he did so. He tucked it into the crook of his arm, and she could feel the warmth of his body from where her hand was snug against it.

It was musty in the space — Rebecca could practically smell the dust they had unsettled when the wall had apparently flipped to allow them into this small alcove. Her mind raced with all of the possibilities as to how and why such a thing would be designed. The estate was built too late for it to have been a priest hole. Perhaps an escape route? Or was it an entrance?

Her brain wasn't being entirely true to her at the moment, however. For overpowering the dusty air was the scent of — well, of a man. Valentine smelled of musk, of leather, of spice that she couldn't put a finger on. It didn't matter that she couldn't see the whole of him. She knew she would be able to sense his very presence in the darkest of rooms.

Never in her life had she seen so masculine, so virile a man. He was not the typical member of the nobility. When his hand had brushed up against hers, it was rough, calloused, the hands of a man who worked with them and not simply by holding a pen.

She breathed in deeply in an attempt to calm herself and chase the thoughts of him from her mind. *He is not for you,* she reminded herself. *He is a duke. A duke who has hired your father. Who is to marry a wealthy noblewoman.* But the closer his body pressed against hers as they made their way up the narrow steps, the more the thought was being crowded from her mind, pushed out by images of the two of them together in an entirely different way.

She was saved from herself when they reached the top of the stairs, a fact that became apparent by the longer landing, at the end of which was a door.

"Well?" he asked, his voice a low rumble in her ear that sent trembles down her spine. "Shall we see what lies at the end of this journey?"

"I can hardly wait," she said, her voice sounding breathy even in her own ears. "But, Valentine…"

"Yes?"

"If the house plans are correct, this should be your own chamber, assuming you reside within the main bedroom."

"Impossible. I am sure I would have noticed a door within my own room."

Rebecca said nothing, not wanting to argue — he had a point, but she couldn't see where else they could be.

He dropped her hand from his arm as he used both hands on the doorknob, needing his shoulder to push open the door, which had obviously not been in use for years now. It finally gave under his forceful shove, and he opened the door into further blackness. Val reached back for Rebecca, taking her hand as they entered the room. A shiver ran down Rebecca's spine, knowing that it was just the two of them somewhere unknown.

She breathed in for a moment as Val crossed the room. The scent was familiar. In fact, it smelled exactly like—

She yelped when something soft brushed against her back, but soon light spilled into the room after Valentine opened the door and she looked around, now realizing why the scent was so familiar.

They were in Valentine's dressing room, his clothing

surrounding them. A shirt had brushed over her back as they walked.

"As I thought," she said, smiling broadly with the knowledge and relief that both her instincts and her memory had been correct. She ignored Val's dark look for a moment, turning around to explore the opening beyond.

"I can understand why you wouldn't have noticed the passage," she said, turning and running her hands over where the seams were. "The door had been papered over — it was why it was difficult to open."

She turned around now to look at him, his frame silhouetted in the light of the door.

"The first duke," she said, biting her lip, "why do you think he built such a passage?"

"I wouldn't know," he said with a shrug and a raised eyebrow as he stepped back into the dressing room closer toward her. "For whatever reason *could* someone create a secret passage to a bedchamber?"

"Perhaps he liked to escape parties when they became rather dreary," she said with a half-smile so that he would know she was teasing, as she matched his step by moving toward him in turn.

"Or maybe he wanted to escape fortune-hunting mothers when hosting balls," he said, coming ever closer.

"He could have been hiding from demanding family members," she suggested, leaving just a couple of feet between them.

"Or," he said, close enough now that he was able to reach out and twist a lock of her hair around his finger, "perhaps there was a maiden he loved, or who he desired, but couldn't have. And so he decided that in order to be together, they would find another way."

Rebecca's breath caught in her throat and she could

barely speak, as the duke's face was so close she could feel the warmth of his breath upon her cheek.

"That is utterly romantic," she finally managed in a low voice, and she could feel his grin against her skin.

"If that is romantic," he said, leaning his forehead in against hers, "what do you think of this?"

In the dim light, the final descent of his lips upon hers sent a shock through Rebecca, though one she eagerly welcomed.

Since he had kissed her late last night, she had lain awake imagining it over many times in her mind, but nothing could quite do it as much justice as the true feeling of his lips upon hers. The only problem was, this pressure from him was not enough. She needed more from him, but she wasn't entirely sure of just what that was, or how to ask for it.

But he knew.

When his tongue probed her lips, she opened to him, in equal parts thrilled and terrified when it swept her mouth. She was thrilled by the sensations that coursed through her at the action; terrified as she had no idea what to do in return.

He didn't seem to mind.

He gripped her tighter against him, his hands sliding up and down the sides of her body, from her shoulders down to her waist and back again. The next time, however, they rounded her hips to cup her bottom, pulling it flush against him. Something very hard, very rigid nudged against her, and Rebecca knew she should push back away from him, should leave this dressing room and find her father once more.

But her instincts told her otherwise. They told her to press farther into him, to take all that he was offering her.

He groaned and wrenched his mouth from hers, taking a

step back away from her, though he kept his hands on her shoulders, holding her in place.

"Rebecca," he said, her name grunted out of his mouth, though whether in praise or in supplication he had no idea. "You... are exquisite."

A strange sense of pride swelled within Rebecca at his words. Which was silly. She had never been a woman to seek out a man's approval — unless it regarded her work.

The fact that a man such as Valentine, a duke who could have whatever and whoever he wanted, would choose to be with *her* — even for just this moment — was nearly incomprehensible.

Perhaps it was best she quit this encounter before she said or did something that would remind him of who she was.

"I, ah, I best be going back," she said, hearing the awkwardness in her tone. "Perhaps I could explore this passage again? For my own interest. Not to use the passage. For I wouldn't be coming to your rooms. Unless, that is, I was assisting my father. Not that, I mean, I would be interested to bring a candle and see more, that's all."

She could have slapped a hand over her face for how idiotic she sounded. One kiss with this man and she had lost all ability to think or speak rationally.

Rebecca wasn't exactly experienced in the ways of men, but she was certainly not a naive innocent girl either.

"You are welcome to explore the passage... any time you'd like," Valentine said with a slow smile, one that warmed her to her very core.

"Yes, I... thank you," was all she managed, and he held out a hand beyond her.

"Why do we not go back the way we came?" he asked. "You shouldn't be seen exiting my bedchamber."

"Of course not," she murmured.

"Allow me to find a candle to light the way," he said,

leaving the dressing room for his chamber, returning in moments.

He held out his arm once more.

"Ready?"

She nodded, hardly trusting her voice.

"Ready."

CHAPTER 12

*V*alentine had never been more pleased to have his friend beside him.

He had fought the idea of a valet for quite some time. But in the end, after realizing the extent of dress that would be required in his role as a duke, he had decided that if there was going to be another person seeing him at his most intimate, dressing him and providing for the care of his person, it was going to be someone he could trust.

Which was why, as he stood in front of the floor-length mirror staring at himself and the man beside him, he had asked one of his closest friends to work for him. He had been somewhat surprised when Archie had agreed.

"Are you sure you want to do this?" Archie Thompkins asked him as he tied his cravat. It had taken some time, but he had finally perfected it after much practice.

"I have to."

"You wouldn't be the first noble to be in debt."

"I would be the first St. Vincent."

"Listen, Val—"

"You don't have to say it, Archie," Valentine said, turning from his friend toward the door. "I already know."

"You obviously don't," Archie said as he finished readying Valentine's clothing for later that evening, "or else you wouldn't be continually trying to prove yourself. You're not Matthew, and you don't have to sacrifice yourself in order to make up for his loss."

Val had no wish to argue any further, but it was more than that — he also had no real argument to make. Archie was right. And yet he owed it to his family.

"I have to do right by them — to do what Matthew would have done." He paused. "If it wasn't for me, he would still be here."

Archie began to argue until Val turned a dark look upon him, causing Archie to throw up his hands.

"All right! I'll say no more. Just promise me you'll think about it."

Val nodded before looking at himself just one more time in the mirror.

"I can dress up as much as I want," he murmured, "but I will never look the part of a nobleman."

"That's a good thing," Archie grunted. "Why would you want to look like one of those fops?"

"I'm beginning to second guess my choice of valet," Val said with a snort. "Isn't he supposed to be the one ensuring I look my best?"

Archie shrugged. "You were the one who asked me."

"So I did," Val said as he good-naturedly cuffed his friend. "I'm off to dinner. If only you could take my place."

"Perhaps I would," Archie said with a wink as he gathered Val's clothing from earlier in the day to have washed and pressed. "The architect's daughter is a mighty fine beauty. Can't say I would mind staring at her through all of those ridiculous courses."

A hard knot began to form deep in Valentine's stomach, and his fist involuntarily clenched. He had to remind himself that Archie had no knowledge of anything that had gone on between him and Rebecca — nor would he have guessed that there would have been.

But Archie knew him as well as any other.

He eyed Valentine knowingly.

"Unless you have already laid claim to her?"

Valentine scoffed. "She's the daughter of the man I have hired to see to my estate and my London home. Of course I would not be dallying with such a woman. I need to find myself a wife who will redeem my family in the eyes of all of the nobility."

Archie shrugged. "That doesn't mean you cannot have your fun with others."

Archie had a point. Valentine wasn't exactly a rake, but he wasn't shy around women either. The thought of simply dallying with Rebecca, however, just didn't sit well with him. Besides that, she didn't seem to be the type of woman one could easily forget after having any sort of relations with her — he should know. He couldn't rid her from his mind after just a couple of kisses.

"I'm going down to dinner," was all he said, walking out the door without looking back at Archie. "Then we will prepare for tomorrow."

THIS WAS NOW the third dinner Rebecca had taken part in at Stonehall Estate, and her nerves were becoming quite fraught at the thought of her father saying the wrong thing, which would divulge the reality of their current circumstance.

Thus far, he had primarily droned on about past projects

— which was by far his favorite topic of conversation, and yet a safe one so long as he didn't suddenly believe he was in the midst of one of those renovations as opposed to those at Stonehall Estate or Wyndham House.

Mrs. St. Vincent far preferred to discuss members of the nobility, though Rebecca wondered whether she knew many of those she insinuated she was great friends with. Not that it mattered to Rebecca *who* one was friends with. In fact, she rather wished she had the chance to have close friends of her own, but she and her father had never stayed long enough in any one location, and if she did make friends, it was usually with noblemen's daughters who enjoyed her company while she was there but would never further any acquaintance. Much like her current situation with the duke and his sister.

Though there was something about Jemima that was rather different from most of the young ladies Rebecca had become acquainted with in the past…

"Are you tired of us yet?" Jemima asked now, leaning over from her seat beside Rebecca.

"Of your family?" Rebecca asked in surprise.

"Why, yes," Jemima said, laughing, then lowered her voice so that no others could hear, though it would be difficult for them to do so over Rebecca's father's droning on or Mrs. St. Vincent's lilting voice. "Surely you must be tired of hearing Mother regale you with all of the ladies she has recently met, and with Valentine's brooding over the fact that he has had the awful misfortune to become a duke."

"Your brother is… interesting," Rebecca said carefully, thinking of all the other emotions that came along with Valentine St. Vincent — ones that she certainly was not going to share with his sister.

"So he is," Jemima said carefully, giving no family secrets away. "I am most fortunate. Most brothers would scoff at my work and suggest that now, as a lady, I might prefer needle-work or water colors."

The pointed look she directed toward her mother explained just where she had heard such sentiments.

"However," she continued, affection filling her face, "Val has been more than understanding. He has provided me all that I have needed, including materials and workspace. But it's more than that," she said, her blue eyes glinting. "He *believes* in me. That, Rebecca, is worth more than you can ever know."

Rebecca nodded slowly, a pang of pain striking within her breast. Even in his more lucid moments, her father was in denial of her work. She knew she possessed *some* skill, but his approval would mean the world to her. To know that her work was not only admired by a world-class architect but by her father — her idol and her tutor — would mean every-thing. Instead, he acted as though she was simply drawing his ideas instead of creating her own.

"I understand," she said, and Jemima must have read the sincerity in her voice for she clapped her hands, just once, excitedly in front of her face and smiled enthusiastically. "I actually have a friend I am very close with who I am sure you would get along well with. Her name is Miss Keswick and she is, of all things, an astronomer."

"An astronomer?" Rebecca repeated, feeling like a dunce.

"It's all right, I wasn't particularly well versed in it before, and Celeste has taught me quite a bit — well, as much as I am interested in knowing," Jemima said. "We have formed a bit of a partnership, I suppose you could say. We discuss our aspirations, our challenges, the difficulty in doing what intrigues us without a proper education nor any hope of being recognized for our ideas."

"You never know," Rebecca said optimistically. "Men might come around one day."

Jemima sighed. "You are pretty, Rebecca, and you seem quite intelligent, but sometimes you just have to accept something as truth instead of holding onto optimism."

"So tell me this," Rebecca said, holding up a finger. "If you make an astounding discovery one day, you will not be able to claim it?"

"Yes and no," Jemima said. "I will try, though my best chance is to do so under my brother's name."

"No!" Rebecca said, loudly enough to capture the attention of others at the table and she calmed slightly.

Jemima smiled. "I agree, it is quite provoking. I will try, though, Rebecca, I promise you that. But first," she raised a glass, "to discoveries!"

As they clinked glasses, Rebecca smiled at Jemima, understanding her completely. She longed for recognition of her work, for people to look at her own designs — not those of her father — and say, "Ah, this must be the work of Rebecca Lambert."

But in order to continue doing what she loved, she would likely have to allow all to think her work was her father's. No one would ever take a woman seriously, let alone hire one.

She longed to be able to tell Jemima of her own passion, to share with her both her successes and failures — to have someone to talk to, to understand her. How amazing it would be to not only have friends of her own but to be able to share with them who she truly was and what drove her.

Although, there was one thing that she certainly could not tell Jemima about, and that was the longings she had for the woman's brother.

The man who was only a duke in name. Who sat there at the end of this long table with the most uncomfortable look on his face as he surveyed the room, who put more effort into avoiding conversation with the rest of them than into actually making them feel comfortable.

Who she knew, behind it all, was warm and passionate and could turn her to liquid with one look.

He caught her eye and before she could even pretend that she hadn't been looking at him, he slowly turned his lip up in a smirk, as though to tell her he knew exactly what she had been thinking.

He held her gaze as he pushed back his chair and rose. "My apologies, but I would ask you all to excuse me. I must turn in early, for there is somewhere I must be tomorrow. I will be out all day, so please do not look for me."

It was Jemima's turn to frown.

"Where could you possibly need to go?" she asked.

"Out," he replied and walked out of the room, leaving the rest of them staring after him.

Rebecca's mind began to race. Where would a man secretly need to go at such a time? There was really only one likely scenario. She hardly wanted to think about it, and yet the thought couldn't help but rush into her mind. Was he going to meet a woman? They weren't far from Hungerford… it was likely they had a tavern. Or even a brothel. Her stomach twisted and for a moment she thought she might lose her recently eaten meal all over the table.

"Are you all right?" Jemima asked, cutting through her thoughts, and Rebecca quickly swallowed down the bile that rose in the back of her throat.

"I am, yes, of course," she said, forcing a smile, telling herself that this was for the best, to put some distance between them. So Valentine desired the company of other women. It didn't matter. It couldn't matter.

But it did.

"Actually, I think perhaps something didn't agree with me," she said, rising herself, Jemima following suit with a worried look.

"Oh, no, I'm so sorry—"

"Nothing at all to be sorry for," Rebecca assured her. "Just my fickle stomach is all. I think I might go lie down for a moment."

"I hope you are well soon," Jemima said worriedly, and Rebecca nodded, slightly guilty about the fact she was lying to her new friend.

"Thank you," she said and slipped from the room.

She did feel sick. But she wasn't going to bed.

She knew she was being ridiculous, that she had no right to be jealous or have any concerns about the duke's actions, but she couldn't help herself.

Tomorrow, Rebecca was going after the duke.

CHAPTER 13

*V*alentine swirled his cloak around his body as he stepped out into the slightly chilled air, the foggy mist quickly enveloping him. He hoped it would clear soon for visibility's sake.

The town of Hungerford was not far — close enough that he needn't ride. Besides that, a brisk walk would likely do him good and clear his head of all thoughts of a certain dark-haired woman with the sultry red lips of a siren and feline eyes.

Archie seemed to sense his mood and said nothing, simply walking beside him as the supportive friend he had been since he and Val were five years old.

Valentine had never considered himself a refined sort of man, nor one with any particular charms. He certainly never had an issue in attracting a woman, but he was fortunate that he drew them to him with his physical attributes rather than his guile.

Rebecca, however, seemed to see beyond his façade and into the man he truly was — a thought that frightened him more than anything. No one saw him for who he was, except Archie and perhaps Jemima. But even she had always seen him just as Valentine, her brother, the one who would protect her, would provide for her, and be there when she needed him.

Rebecca was different. Not just from all of the people who were close to him, but from any woman he had met. She asked questions that cut deeply to the heart of the matter, was perceptive and observant. When she looked at him, it was as though she could see beyond what he presented to the world and through to his deepest thoughts. It was unnerving.

It also made him want to strip her bare and have *her* be the vulnerable one.

At any rate... today he had to forget all of that. Forget about her. And focus on his plan. Step one to save himself from debt — make himself easy money.

"Do you think anyone will be here from the *ton* and recognize you as the Duke of Wyndham?" Archie asked, finally breaking the silence.

"No," Val shook his head. "Those who know me from Hungerford will see me as a different man from any who might be here from London. You have everything we need?"

"Of course," Archie said, eyeing him with a look of contempt that Val would think to question him.

"Just making sure."

"You don't want to return to London to do this?"

"I'm more likely to be recognized in London. They consider me as one of the Fancy there, and the other nobles have seen me box. Besides that, you know as well as I do that the greatest matches aren't held there. You know the nobles — they love the idea, but as soon as they might get their hands dirty or a bit of true danger shows its ugly face, they disdain it."

"You don't need to tell me that," Archie said with a shrug.

"And after my last fight in London…"

"I understand," Archie said, and Valentine was as grateful as always to have a man with him who he didn't need to explain himself to. "What do you think of Brown? Will you be ready for him? You've been training with fine gentlemen, a far cry from those who fight knowing that all is on the line."

"I'm ready for whatever — or whoever — comes at me," Valentine said confidently. He might not believe he was the right man to become Duke of Wyndham, but here, he had no qualms.

"This will be something of a trial run," Archie continued. "If you win this, well then, there could be bigger fights — bigger purses. But your name would become better known. Can't say I've ever heard of any duke fighting beyond Jackson's."

"I don't need a bigger fight," Valentine said quietly. "Just this one. This purse — for now."

"Ah, right, and then you're going to marry your fancy lady and run your estates," Archie said.

"Is that a bit of sarcasm I sense in your tone?"

Archie just smiled as they continued.

"A good bit of luck, that Stonehall is so close to Hunger-ford," Archie said with a half-grin.

"I always knew we were family of the duke's… I just didn't know how close."

"You know, it won't go over well, a duke walking away with the prize money," Archie said, shaking his head.

"It's a nothing match," Valentine countered. "It will hardly attract any attention."

But just then they came atop the crest of a hill, and below them, they could see horses and carriages lining the field.

"My God," Valentine said, his mouth hanging open. "What are all of these people doing here?"

They pushed through the crowd to the center of the field, where a man greeted them without a note of recognition, as Valentine pulled his hat low over his eyes. Archie introduced him as Val Vincent, which was the name he had fought under previously in an attempt to distance himself from his family, who were not exactly approving — and they had turned out to be right.

"Bucky Brown here?"

The man nodded.

"Best to keep the two of you separate until you're ready. Come, I'll find space for you to prepare yourself."

Val nodded, and the two of them followed.

His heart was already beginning to pound rapidly, his adrenaline rushing through his veins. This was what he lived for. This was who he was. He had tried to give it up, especially when it had nearly cost him everything, but he was as addicted to this as many men were to drink.

He could hardly wait to get into the ring.

* * *

WHAT IN THE... Rebecca could hardly believe what she was seeing, as she followed Valentine and his valet. People milled about, seemingly from every walk of life. There were some dressed much finer than she, others dressed in what were clearly working clothes. Music filled the air, though from where Rebecca had no idea. There must be musicians hidden somewhere in the crowd. Open carriages lined what appeared to be a common green, while country people poured in from every direction.

What was Valentine doing here?

Everyone seemed to be clustered around the one main area, and Rebecca inched ever closer, twisting herself this way and that to try to get through the crowd of people to see what was happening. The grass was wet under her boots, the ground miry from the multitudes of feet that had recently tread upon it.

As she attempted to keep herself from being pushed over, Rebecca looked around her with rapt attention, unable to tear her eyes away. In the midst of the melee was untrampled grass, near glistening in the noonday sun. A man drew a long stick through the dirt in the middle of the ropes that hung from the stakes that had been embedded into the ground.

She said a prayer that this wasn't some kind of animal fight. She couldn't bear to watch such a thing, and she hoped that wasn't what Valentine was here for. Then a man stood on a box and started shouting rules to the crowd, of what they could and couldn't do. He pointed out a bag of money hanging from the stake farthest away from Rebecca. Then he called out the names, "Bucky Brown and Val Vincent!"

Val Vincent. Rebecca's jaw dropped open and just then a man entered from the opposite side, flanked by two men. This must be Bucky Brown.

Then, from the nearer side, entered Valentine with his valet and another man. Valentine's beautiful body was bare from the waist up, for he was dressed only in his breeches, his back glistening in the bright sun which had burned away the earlier fog. She didn't even have time to admire him as she was both captivated and horrified by all that was happening and what she realized was about to come.

Valentine and his opponent — Brown, Rebecca reminded herself — each stood on one side of the line, toe-to-toe as they stared one another down before quickly shaking hands.

Despite the rapid beat of her heart that seemed to be hitting the very wall of her chest, Rebecca couldn't help but note that the two of them looked like a pair of Greek statues, so chiseled, so poised as they stood just as still. Finally, they

ELLIE ST. CLAIR

broke away, backing up ever so slightly as they each raised their bare fists in front of them.

"Fight!" the man yelled.

The two pugilists circled each other before each feinted a couple of punches, the other ducking or dashing out of the way. Then Brown's fist hit Val's chest, and Rebecca cringed with the impact. They continued to exchange blows on the soft, fleshy parts of themselves before Brown hit Valentine's jaw with a resounding crack and then connected with his cheekbone. Blood began pouring down Val's face and into his eye.

Rebecca heard a scream and didn't realize until moments later that it was her own. Then Valentine, fortunately, lifted his hands in front of him, creating a guard that prevented Brown from coming close again.

They went back and forth, neither striking any great blows until Brown aimed a shot that almost hit Val's neck; but instead, Val quickly blocked it and then struck a fist into Brown's cheekbone, drawing a rush of blood. Brown staggered for a moment before collapsing to the ground, and Rebecca held her breath, but he was soon helped back up before the two of them returned to opposite corners of the ring.

Rebecca needed the time to compose herself as much as the fighters did. She had never seen such violence up close. While she knew she had been rather shielded, she could hardly believe that Valentine actually *enjoyed* such a sport.

The next two rounds were fairly uneventful, though Brown did not look quite as strong as he once had — Val's last punch had proven to knock some of the bluster from him.

After a couple of rounds, however, Brown regained some of his enthusiasm, and the men began to trade full, powerful blows. The more their faces bled and their knuckles cracked, the sicker Rebecca became. Until suddenly, despite the fact one of his eyes was only half open, Val's gaze seemed to catch hers. Rebecca could only stare as he looked at her in astonishment, and then suddenly their connection broke with a crack — Brown's fist connected so solidly with Valentine's nose that he went down like a sack of potatoes.

Tears began to fill Rebecca's eyes as she sank back into the crowd of people, who were happy to push around her so they would have a better view themselves. She heard another crack but didn't see what had happened, for she had averted her eyes, unable to watch anymore. She knew she was being ridiculous, but the thought that Val — beautiful, passionate Val — was subjecting himself to such a terrible sport for the entertainment of the blood-hungry crowd and a few coins nearly tore her apart.

Until finally she was out of the crowd and into the open air, where she took deep breaths to calm herself.

So this was what he *had* to do. She wondered if she would prefer his visit to Hungerford was for the purpose of finding a woman. Would that have been better? For then at least he would be doing something beautiful, even if it were not with her.

This did explain so much. Why his father had been disappointed in him, why he so hated his new role of duke. If this was what fueled him, then his new life would have no room for it, would not coincide. For as much as the nobility, particularly the Fancy, treated men such as fighters as though they were to be celebrated, prizefighters themselves were not of the noble class. It just wasn't done.

Rebecca couldn't stay and watch. Yet she couldn't leave either. Not until she knew what had happened, how Val was. So she crouched on her heels in a miserable ball at the outskirts of the crowd for what felt like hours.

Until finally the people seemed to turn as one and she had

to scurry out of the way to avoid being trampled. She waited, not altogether patiently, for Val to appear, but he didn't come. Once she was sure the middle field had to be empty, that most had departed, she hesitantly walked toward it.

And brought her hand to her throat at the sight before her.

CHAPTER 14

*V*al had no idea how he had gotten home. The last thing he had remembered was seeing Rebecca's face in the crowd. Then Brown's fist had intervened and everything had gone black. How many rounds had he gone?

He tried to pry open an eye, but only a crack of light filtered in for a moment. Then something very wet and cold was dropped upon it and he could no longer see at all.

"Archie, take the bloody cloth off my eye," he ordered, though what he had meant to come out in a commanding tone sounded more like a weak groan.

"Archie is not here at the moment," came a silky, feminine voice.

"Rebecca?" He really wished she wasn't here right now — this was not exactly how he would wish a woman to see him.

"You are covered in blood, gashes, and bruises," she said, though her tone was far from sympathetic but rather accusatory. "What were you thinking?"

"Just another day making a living," he mumbled as he sat up. He refused to lie there like an invalid.

He reached up, pulling the cold cloth off his eye, and he

was able to open it slightly wider. He looked around him, recognizing the gold motifs on the wall as those from his sitting room. Old family portraits of years past, featuring people who were so distant relatives they hardly mattered stared back at him as though they were judging him. He was reclined on the worn red chesterfield, while Rebecca sat on her knees on the floor next to him.

"I'm back at Stonehall?"

"You are," she said, wringing out a piece of linen in a bowl of water — very red, bloody water. His blood, obviously. "Thanks to your valet. Or should I call him your second?"

"He's my friend."

"Yes, well, he had to walk all the way home to fetch a horse. Were you honestly so sure of yourself that you thought you would be able to walk home?"

Yes, he had been, but he wasn't entirely sure how to tell her that at the moment.

"I suppose I lost, then?"

One corner of her lip twitched, and he sensed that she would have liked to have laughed at him, but was still angry. Though, he thought with a twinge of ire himself, what he chose to do with his time shouldn't matter to her. He was a fighter — always had been — and if she didn't like that, well, she should leave him be.

"Yes, you most certainly lost."

"I never lose."

"You did today."

"It was your fault."

"What?" her hazel-green eyes flew up to meet his. "How in the world could this possibly be *my* fault?"

"I saw you."

"I wasn't there."

"Don't lie to me," he said, and her eyes narrowed in response, though she said nothing. "You were there, in the crowd. I saw you and I was distracted. Brown would never have bested me otherwise."

"You think highly of yourself."

"I *know* that I am a skilled fighter. It's what I do. It's who I am."

"Do you enjoy it?"

He was about to answer that yes, of course he enjoyed it. But then he paused for a moment. *Did* he enjoy it?

He enjoyed the thrill that rushed through him. He liked using his body, the physical exertion of it. He loved being good at something, knowing there was something he was proficient at, could excel at.

Except he hadn't. Not tonight. And it crushed him.

"It's part of me," he answered her, lifting the cloth from her hand and wiping the scrape on his cheek, though he rubbed it too hard and winced at the sting of it.

"Don't be so stubborn," she said, taking the cloth back and wiping his brow once more. He had to admit that it was nice to be cared for, though he wasn't about to tell her that.

"Why were you there?" he asked, propping himself up on an elbow to better see her, but she dipped her gaze sideways to the bowl on the long table in the middle of the room.

"I told you I wasn't."

"Rebecca."

She sniffed, not entirely pleased about answering him.

"I was curious."

"Of the match? How did you know about it?"

She was silent, and he could tell that she was holding something back from him, not interested in sharing.

Finally, she sighed and flung the linen down in exasperation as she looked up at him.

"I was following you, all right? I wanted to know what would be so pressing that you had to go into the village. I thought… I thought…"

"You thought what?" he asked, more gently now in the hopes that his tone would encourage her to speak.

"I thought you were going to find a woman," she mumbled, her words almost so indiscernible that he could hardly hear them.

"Say that again?"

"I'd rather not."

He grinned now, inordinately pleased. She was jealous — not that she wanted to admit it.

"I really didn't hear you," he lied.

She glared up at him, her eyes shooting daggers.

"I *said* that I thought you were going to town to find a woman."

"And you thought to follow me... to do what?" He couldn't help it. His body began to shake.

"Do *not* laugh at me!"

"I'm sorry," he said, the mirth bubbling up through him and out his cracked lip. "I can't help it."

"It's not funny!" she protested, her brow furrowed as she stared at him.

"Actually, it is."

"How could that be possible?"

"Rebecca," he said, reaching out and cupping her chin in his hand, careful not to allow any of his cuts to bloody her face. "Why would I go seek out another woman when I have one as beautiful as you currently residing in my house?"

She eyed him.

"Perhaps you were going to look for a woman with loose morals."

He shook his head.

"I couldn't — for another woman would never do, as I would only be picturing you."

"I really wish you wouldn't say such beautiful things to me."

He tilted his head to study her. "You think my words are beautiful? That's the first time anyone has said such a thing about me, I think. I usually bungle it all up."

"I find," she said, sitting up on her knees now and resting her elbows on his chest as he tried not to wince, "that if you say the simple truth of the matter, it works best."

"I'll remember that," he said, smiling at her.

"Your face truly looks terrible," she said with the smallest of smiles.

"Now those words are not particularly lovely," he retorted.

"Who said I was trying to charm you?" she lifted an eyebrow, and her impish grin seemed to heal all of the pain that had emanated from his cuts and bruises moments ago.

He laughed. "You have charmed me without even trying."

"So you think."

At that moment, he wanted — no, *needed* — to kiss her. It didn't matter that it might hurt. No pain could be worse than the restraint of keeping himself from her.

He lifted his hand around the back of her head, drawing it down toward him. She looked hesitant for a moment, focusing on what he knew must be his wreck of a face, but she relented, allowing him to pull her head down to his. Her kiss was tender, light, and just what he needed.

Until it wasn't enough. He pushed himself up to a sitting position, then reached down to lift her onto the couch on top of him, so that she was straddling his lap. With enough pressure on her lips, he no longer felt any pain, for the pleasure and desire that coursed through him at her proximity chased it all away.

She, however, hadn't forgotten.

"Am I not hurting you?"

"Far from it," he said, pulling her closer toward him,

needing her warmth, her healing presence. "You, Rebecca, could never hurt me."

"I hardly think that's true," she said, her hands coming to his face, running over the cuts and bruises that he knew would only look worse tomorrow. "Does your head not hurt you? You must have taken quite the hit, though I wouldn't know, for I didn't stay to see it."

"Oh, yes, you were running away by that point."

"I could hardly watch you be beaten so."

"Excuse me, but I believe I was the one doing just as much of the beating."

"Which was equally hard to watch."

He twined his fingers through her hair, pulling out the pins that he found holding it up on the back of her head, loving the silky tresses spiraling out over his hands. So soft, so sweet in comparison to his own brutishness.

"You care for me," he stated, to which she set her lips in a firm line.

"I never said that."

"But you do."

"Perhaps I simply do not enjoy violence."

He shrugged. "Be that as it may, you don't seem overly concerned for Brown."

"I shouldn't be concerned for either of you." She sighed. "For it was your own foolish decision to take part."

He smirked at her as he drew her face closer toward him, her hair now floating freely about her shoulders.

"Admit you care," he whispered in her ear.

"No," she said, though her words came out near to a moan.

He began kissing his way down her neck, over the soft skin behind her perfectly formed ear.

"Say it," he commanded softly.

"I'd rather not," she said, but she arched her head to the side so that he could better access her neck.

He continued kissing a trail downward until finally, he reached the skin just above her bodice.

"Are you sure you wouldn't like to?" he asked, teasing a finger over the material, inching it down ever so slowly. He circled her nipple with a finger but refused to give her what she wanted, despite the fact that she was arching her chest toward him, likely without even realizing she was doing so.

"Fine," she finally bit out, her eyes nearly closed now, her head tilted slightly backward. "I care. A bit."

He chuckled lowly at her stubbornness and refusal to tell him the full truth of it, but he relented, freeing her breast and tweaking the nipple between his fingers before lowering his mouth and tasting her.

She moaned, her sigh long and soft, stirring his loins in a way that no woman had in quite some time.

She shifted on his lap, and he nearly went wild in anticipation. He wanted her with a ferocity he could hardly put into words. Both the best and the worst part of it all? He could tell she felt the same.

For he knew he could have her right here and now.

But he was also very aware that he shouldn't.

He couldn't promise her anything beyond this moment in time. She was the daughter of an architect, a man of means, but not the means that Valentine was looking for. It made him feel like a whore himself at the fact that he was marrying for money, but he couldn't see any other way around it.

Clearly, he wasn't getting anywhere prizefighting anymore.

"What's wrong?" she asked softly, her hands cupping his face.

"Nothing," he said, chasing away the thoughts from his mind.

"Are you sure?"

"Of course," he said. "What more could I ask for than the most beautiful woman I have ever seen writhing on my lap?"

"I am not *writhing!*"

"Oh, I would argue otherwise."

She laughed then as she ran her hands over his face, feeling the broken bridge of his nose, his rough eyebrows, his prominent cheekbones.

He closed his eyes, giving himself over to her cooling touch.

"It's not exactly a work of art," he said, but when he opened his eyes he saw her shaking her head.

"I would argue otherwise," she said. "Your face is one of character. One that tells a story. It's what I love best about buildings such as Stonehall, which are hundreds of years old. This estate holds so much life within it that it speaks to me in a way others do not."

"To you?" he asked, confused, but she chose that moment to lean in and kiss him once more. His last coherent thought was that she must have come to appreciate architecture and buildings after living with her father, the architect, for so long. He chose then to simply revel in the sweet passion of her kiss.

Her face grew hazy then, and while he didn't think he had closed his eyes, his world started to go black, and he began to lose even the sensation of her lips upon his.

"Val?" he heard, but her voice seemed to be far away in the distance.

Then everything went dark.

CHAPTER 15

"*I*s something the matter?" Jemima whispered to Rebecca at the breakfast table, but she shook her head. She had been awaiting Valentine's appearance for the past quarter of an hour.

Last night after he had passed out she had summoned Archie, but he hadn't seemed overly concerned.

"Just a result of a few hits to the head," he had said nonchalantly. Understanding the situation, however, he had suggested that Rebecca might want to retire, and he would see to his friend and employer.

"Not to worry," he had told her. "Isn't the first time Val has been knocked out for the night."

But worry she did. She had hardly slept through the night, so concerned was she, and this morning she had been eager to see what condition Valentine was in when she entered the breakfast room.

"Not at all," she answered Jemima's question now on whether anything was wrong, though her new friend eyed her with some suspicion. Rebecca was unsure what she was supposed to say, however. That her father sat through their sessions droning on and on about previous projects with ever-decreasing input on their current project while she did it all on her own? That she had to determine just how they were going to make back all of the money he had lost, while not ruining their reputation with the row of houses he had built on speculation, of which all were now sitting empty in London? That the man she was falling for, Jemima's brother, had no room in his life for her besides what would be a brief dalliance, and might now be lying in his room with a head injury?

There was nothing she could exactly share at the moment. So, she did what she always did and fixed a smile on her face as she moved the food around her plate to make it look as though she had eaten something, for she couldn't stomach anything right now.

"Good morning. Apologies for my tardiness."

"Valentine!"

They all turned toward the door to see Val walk in, but it was his mother's exclamation that rose above the rest of them. He did look truly awful this morning. Both eyes were surrounded by a sickly shade of yellow and green, his scratches were pronounced on his pale face, and his gait was slightly pained.

But he picked up his plate and began to load it from the sideboard as though nothing was amiss.

His mother waited until he sat down to address him.

"My God, Valentine, what are you thinking?"

Apparently she was aware of what would cause such injuries.

"Nothing to worry about, Mother," he said, waving a hand in the air. "Just a friendly little bout, is all."

"Valentine, if that is friendly, I should hate to see any animosity," Jemima said. Rebecca could hardly enter the conversation, for she didn't want to admit to being anywhere near the fight. Valentine looked her way for a moment, however, and sent her a quick wink that, fortunately, everyone else missed, so intent were they on what had happened.

"Why, Valentine?" his mother said, resting her cutlery on the table as she brought her hands to her face dramatically. "You are a *duke* now. It is one thing to go have fun with other noblemen at that place you all attend, but I cannot imagine there is anywhere near here for you to do such a thing."

"There is not," he said, tucking into his food as though nothing was amiss. "To answer your question, I did it for the purse."

"Did you win?"

At that, he paused with a forkful of food halfway to his mouth. "I did not."

"Then it wasn't even worth it," his mother mourned, shaking her head. "That beautiful face, and you would throw it all away for a bag of prize money. I suppose there is nothing a man wouldn't do for a heavy purse."

Rebecca's head shot up at Mrs. St. Vincent's words — though not for how they currently related to the situation. No, they had triggered something in Rebecca's mind. An idea, that could potentially make all the difference to her own financial situation.

"What is it?" Jemima asked her now, though after a moment her eyes widened as she stared at Rebecca in surprise. "You knew."

"Pardon?" Rebecca pretended to misunderstand her.

"You knew that Val fought yesterday, or at least of his current condition. You were not indisposed, as we all thought."

She spoke softly enough so that no one else at the table could hear, but still, Rebecca looked around them to make sure that no one was within hearing range.

"I, ah, I did happen to see him yesterday, yes," she said, not wanting to lie to Jemima but also not inclined to share the entire situation. "I thought it was, however, his circumstance to share."

"We are quite the unconventional lot, aren't we?" Jemima said with a chuckle. "You have likely never seen any such as us before."

"Every family has their quirks," Rebecca answered diplomatically.

At which time her father rose from the table and walked out of the room. The rest of them stared after his unexcused exit for a moment before turning to Rebecca.

"I, ah, excuse me, please, I best go ensure he is well," she said with a forced smile before hastily pushing back her chair and following him out the door.

"Father!" she called, chasing after him as he strode through the ante-room before entering the long gallery.

"Yes?" he said, finally turning at her voice, though his eyes held that faraway look that caused her such despair.

"What are you doing?" she asked, her breath coming in huffs once she finally caught up to him. "We were in the midst of breakfast."

"A man can choose when to leave in his own home," he said indignantly, and Rebecca brought a hand to the back of her neck as tension began to form.

"But Father... this is not your house," she said, though she knew her words were futile. It was usually simply a matter of time before he returned to himself. She took his hand and led him over to the sofa. Perhaps a change of subject, an idea that could potentially solve their problems, might capture his attention.

"Father, do you recall the houses you recently built? The ones on Atticus Street?"

"Yes, of course," he said indignantly. "Some of my finest work. How could I not remember?"

Rebecca took a deep breath, reminding herself not to be hurt by his accusatory tone. He didn't understand why she would ask him such a thing.

"I had a thought for how we might be able to make back the money invested into them."

"They will sell because they are the finest of buildings, some of the most beautiful in London."

"Yes, of course, they are," she placated him, knowing he wouldn't listen to reason — that they were too unconventional and, as a result, too expensive, for most to purchase. Besides that, they were too far from London's fashionable West End. "But I was thinking, perhaps the best way to showcase how truly wonderful they are would be to hold a lottery."

"A lottery?"

"Yes," she said, warming to her idea now. "The prize would be the houses themselves. People would enjoy the idea of possibly winning. With the lottery, they could buy tickets and then potentially end up with, as you say, one of the finest homes in London."

She looked at him expectantly.

"What do you think?"

"It would certainly bring many people to see my work," he said thoughtfully. "And then we can finish the development."

"Yes," she agreed. "And the best part of it is that truly anyone could win."

"That will also be the greatest issue, Rebecca," he said, frowning. "There will be some who won't want just anyone living in a fine London neighborhood. In fact, we will likely require approval."

"From who?"

"I'm not entirely sure," he admitted. "But it required

approval to demolish the original structures and rebuild. We shall think on it."

"Well, we have a couple of weeks or so before we return to London," she said, rubbing the back of her neck. "Which reminds me — we must work hard on these plans if we'd like to have a draft completed before we go."

"Very well," he said with a wave of his hand. "Carry on."

* * *

So carry on Rebecca did. Her father had retired early that evening, and once more she was alone in the long gallery. It was interesting, she reflected, how in the dark of night what was an innocent vase or painting during the day was made sinister. All sorts of wild thoughts entered one's mind after the clock struck midnight and no one was about.

At that thought, she heard a footstep in the distance. There is no such thing as ghosts, she told herself, rolling her eyes at the fact that the thought had even crossed her mind.

She was a practical woman, not given to the fanciful, she reminded herself as she heard the footsteps approaching.

Which was also a reason why she had to stay far from the duke. For if that was him out in the hall…

"Rebecca."

It was.

She scrambled to her feet, once more shoving her papers underneath one of the few large books she had been consulting.

"Your grace— that is, Valentine. What are you doing here?"

"I must admit that I was actually hoping I would find you here. You must be one of those people who craves the long night hours."

She would actually prefer to be in bed. It was simply that

she didn't have much choice. If she was to finish this and to do so without the rest of them guessing who was actually designing their homes, then night it was.

Unless Valentine continued to make a habit of interrupting her.

"Sometimes," was all she said when she realized he was awaiting her reply. "And you?"

He shrugged. "Sometimes," he repeated her, causing her to smile at him.

"Listen," he said, taking more steps toward her. "I sought you out to apologize."

"For what?" she asked, her heart beating ever faster as he stopped before her and took her hand in his.

"For, well, for fainting on you. Archie was quite chagrined with me when I came to."

"I didn't know who else to seek out."

"You were correct, he was the best choice," Val said, walking over to the sideboard and pouring himself a drink from the one bottle they currently had in the room — whiskey, her father's favorite.

"How often has that happened to you?" she asked curiously.

"That I've been beaten?"

"That you have lost consciousness."

"Oh. Ah... four or five times now."

"Why do you look so unconcerned?" she asked, aghast at his nonchalance.

"I am always fine afterward. Though it seems to be happening more often now — nearly every good hit to the head results in it. At any rate, I didn't want you to think that I had fainted as a result of your touch."

Despite her concern for him, Rebecca couldn't help a bit of mirth at his expense. The thought that a man his size, so masculine, so physically obvious, would faint at the mere touch of her lips...

"What?" he said, furrowing his brow.

"Nothing," she said, but a near-giggle slipped out.

"You're laughing at me."

"I am not."

He raised an eyebrow. "I believe you are."

"Fine," she said, the laughter spilling out now. "It's just the thought that you could go rounds being punched in the face but then think that I would believe that I could fell with you one kiss... why, it is rather humorous."

He finally broke a grin himself and chuckled slightly. "I see your point."

"Although," she swallowed her fear and took a step closer to him, "there is only one way to prove that was not the cause."

"Oh?" he said, setting his drink down, his eyes becoming quite hooded as he lost all humor and returned her stare. "And just what would that be?"

"To try it again, of course," she said, and he nodded slowly.

"That, Rebecca, is an excellent idea."

He reached out and ran his hands along her bare arms until they locked around her hands, and then he slowly began to tug her toward him, until she was but a breath away.

"I think, if we are going to recreate this correctly, it was you who had kissed me," he said slyly, and Rebecca's breath caught in her throat. It was one thing to have kissed him when they were already in the midst of passion, but to be the aggressor from the outset...

Well, she best get to it.

She closed her eyes, leaned in, and pressed her lips against his.

Rebecca had thought that their kiss last night was the best she would ever have.

She was wrong.

Last night he had obviously only been semi-lucid. Today, with all of his faculties intact, he was something else entirely.

He kissed like he fought. She may have been the one to initiate the kiss, but he soon took over, thrusting and parrying without restraint. His tongue sought hers, caressing yet also promising what would await her should they go any further than this.

She moaned at the onslaught, her hands coming up to grip his shoulders as though she were drowning and he was her only chance of salvation.

When he tore his lips from hers, she sagged against him, entirely at his mercy.

He tilted her chin up to look at him. "See? Still lucid."

She nodded jerkily. "I, however, am not."

"Forgive me."

"There is nothing to forgive."

She looped her arms around his neck, now as desperate as he was. She needed more of him, wanted to be close to him. She was well aware that their time together would be brief. She knew that there was nothing for them in the future. But could she not have this moment in time with him? Being with him brought her close to someone in a way that she had never been before, nor likely ever would again. Why could she not have this with him, however fleeting it might be?

A small voice deep inside told her she shouldn't allow it, for then she would only want more.

But his lips upon hers silenced that voice completely.

It was Rebecca who pushed his jacket off his shoulders. It was she who slipped the buttons of his shirt from their holes before lifting it over his head. It was also she who unfastened his trousers, though she wasn't quite brave enough to actually slip them off.

Power coursed through her when his breathing became ragged. This giant of a man who would go toe-to-toe in battle with another fighter was so supple in her arms. She ran her fingers over the bruises on his chest and he didn't even wince.

"Do these not hurt?" she asked, hearing the huskiness in her voice.

"Not as long as you don't press too hard," he said with a low chuckle.

She couldn't help herself. She pushed ever-so-gently on one of them.

He growled.

"Did you just growl?" she asked, her eyes wide.

He pinched her bottom.

"Ouch!"

His eyes glittered. "How do you like that?"

She narrowed her eyes at him, but before she could utter another word he had swept her up in his arms and deposited her on the sofa next to them. He ran his hands up and down her sides before he lowered them, lifting her skirts and slowly beginning to run his hand up her leg. She shivered involuntarily at his touch.

His fingers crept even higher still until they were near to circling the very center of her, and she found herself arching toward him, wanting more.

When he finally stroked her, she nearly jumped off the couch. He smiled wickedly.

"And how does that feel?" he murmured in her ear.

"Better than a pinch."

He chuckled once more, the low timbre of his voice amplifying the thrills that were already coursing through her from his touch.

"Very well then," he said.

She reached for him, but he stilled her hand.

"This is for you," he said. "Let someone do something for you, for once."

His words caused her to stop for a moment. He was right, she realized. She couldn't remember the last time she had surrendered and allowed someone to do something for her instead of the other way around.

So she let go — she threw her head back and gave herself over to the sensations of his fingers on her center, his mouth and his other hand on her breasts. She was climbing higher and higher toward something, and she knew instinctively that she wanted to reach that pinnacle with him.

She tugged at his trousers once more, and he caught her hands in his.

"Are you sure?" he asked, his words stilted, his breathing ragged.

"More than anything," she managed. "You are right about one thing. I should do something that I want, make a memory that I will always cherish. And I want to do that with you."

His expression was both pained and ecstatic, if it were possible.

"I don't know…"

"Please?"

CHAPTER 16

She could have no idea what she was currently doing to him. For he didn't believe she was that cruel, to torture him on the highest order. He knew that while she wasn't a lady in title, she was one in every other way. He shouldn't take her on the sofa, as a one-time event. It wasn't right. It wasn't done.

But the way she was looking at him, with such pleading on her face, was his undoing. He asked her once more if she was sure, and the glare she sent his way said more than words.

He was sunk.

He buried his hands in her long, silky dark tresses, which rippled over his fingers like water. He tasted her once more before dipping a finger into her lush folds to ensure she was ready for him. It took him but moments to rid himself of his trousers and her of her dress and chemise, leaving nothing between them. He positioned himself between her legs, finding her arching up toward him, more than eager.

"Are you ready?" he asked in a guttural tone, and she

nodded, one of her long, soft hands coming up to cup his cheek.

He guided himself into her slowly, but she lifted herself up toward him so that they were joined much swifter than he would have imagined.

"Rebecca!" he moaned her name at her sharp intake of breath, but when he pried his eyes open, hers were clear and free of pain.

"I'm fine," she said.

Yet he couldn't help but ask, "Are you sure?"

"If you ask me that one more time, I am going to punch you myself," she threatened, and if he could have laughed, he would have, but at the moment he could do nothing but focus on keeping himself in control.

He was trying to give her time to adjust to him, to stretch to fit him, but when she began moving, he was lost. He began to pump into her in a rhythm as old as time itself, though Valentine didn't think it had ever been so perfect between a man and woman before.

Knowing he couldn't keep himself from finding fulfillment much longer, he reached down between them and began to stroke her until she was trembling around him, squeezing him even tighter than she had been before.

He just managed to pull himself from her before expending himself onto his shirt next to her. Replete, he had only enough energy to sink down onto the sofa next to her, drawing her into his arms. She lay her head on his chest, and he lifted his jacket to place it over top of her.

Guilt began to creep into his soul.

"That was poorly done of me," he said, looking around them. "Your first time should have been on your marriage bed — or, at the very least, on a bed, for goodness sake. I am sure that is what a proper duke would have done. I, however—"

"You are magnificent."

He snorted. "I would hardly say that is a fitting description."

"Were you on the other side of this encounter?"

"I suppose not."

"Then you will have to trust me. It was... more than I ever could have asked for."

Her serene smile finally convinced him, and he held her closer toward him, closing his eyes, basking in the moment. If only he could hold her like this forever — for he didn't see how, after her, another woman would ever do.

He rested his chin on her head and closed his eyes.

Then drifted off to sleep.

* * *

LIGHT BEGAN to filter through Rebecca's eyelids, which was rather odd. She typically closed the drapes tightly against the outside, whether she was at home or here at Stonehall Estate. Her room was rather sumptuous, if dated. The heavy brocade navy curtains kept the room quite dark, just as she liked it for sleep, but the cream walls and large windows allowed for the light and beautiful view of the hills beyond to filter in and bring the lightness to her soul that she always strove for when designing.

She opened her eyes and gasped. She wasn't in her room.

She heard a snore.

And she wasn't alone.

"Valentine," she hissed, shaking him, and he groggily opened his eyes as well.

"Rebecca?" His eyes focused. "Rebecca!"

She looked around her furtively to ensure no one was about, and then leaped off him and began to hurriedly dress in her chemise and her gown.

"I cannot believe we fell asleep!" she exclaimed, though she kept her voice just above a whisper, for if there was light it would mean, at the very least, servants were already about.

"Well, it *was* rather late," he said, swinging his legs over the edge of the sofa and rubbing his eyes.

Rebecca paused for a moment, unable to miss the opportunity to catch a glimpse of his magnificent body.

He ran a hand through his hair, seemingly unconcerned. It wasn't as though the sofa had been overly comfortable. It had just been so comforting to be held, to give herself over to someone else for once.

But now she was suffering the consequences for that.

Thankfully she was used to readying herself alone, and she was able to slip the larger buttons through their holes without his help. While he had been of assistance last night to undress her, a look at his sizeable hands, still swollen from his fight, had her wondering whether or not he would be of any help this morning.

"Val?"

Rebecca froze in the midst of her dressing, her eyes meeting Valentine's, and he jumped to his feet, though when he did he was fully naked once more. And, she noticed, erect.

He followed her gaze and then shrugged with a smirk, and she rolled her eyes at him.

"Seriously?" she hissed. His sister called his name again from out in the hall in search of him, and then Rebecca heard her father.

"Miss St. Vincent, good morning." His voice carried through the door. At least he knew who Jemima was this morning. Sometimes he didn't, though Rebecca always managed to cover his forgetfulness. "Have you seen my daughter yet?"

"I haven't," she replied, her voice still far down the hall but coming closer. "She must have slept late."

"May I escort you down the hall to breakfast?"

"That would be lovely."

"Jemima!" Oh, goodness, it was Mrs. St. Vincent now. Her voice certainly had Valentine moving, as he began to gather all of his clothes in his arms.

"Aren't you going to put them on?" Rebecca whispered.

"There isn't time," he murmured back. "Besides, if I do manage to get them on, I'll just look as disheveled as you and that certainly won't help anything."

"Neither will the two of us being found in here with you completely naked!"

Then she was suddenly reminded of something. "Through the passage!" She crossed the room in a few quick strides, waving him over. "Hurry!"

"Rebecca will likely be awaiting me in the long gallery," came her father's voice, just steps away now, and Val sprinted across the room. Rebecca grabbed the shelf, and just as footsteps drew near, the wall turned and they were on the other side.

They looked at one another, utterly relieved, and began to laugh. Rebecca fell in his arms and Valentine kissed the top of her head.

"Now," he said, after taking her hand and drawing her up the stairs where he pushed open the dressing room door, "what do you say we—"

Rebecca peered around him to see what had brought a halt to his words.

There stood Archie through the door of the dressing room.

"Well," he said, his blue eyes lighting up and a smile stretching across his face. "Good morning, *your grace*. Miss Lambert. Now, just where have the two of you been?"

His eyes flicked up and down Val's naked body, and Rebecca heaved a sigh of relief that, at the very least, her clothes were on, as wrinkled and disheveled as they may be.

"I'll, ah, I'll just be going then," she said, edging around Valentine and then Archie, but Archie took some pity on her and held up a finger.

"Just a moment, Miss Lambert," he said. "Let me see if there is anyone about."

Rebecca could have told them that everyone was currently downstairs, but she supposed there could be a servant or two in the corridor. Archie looked outside, then held the door open for her.

"All is clear," he said, and then nodded at her, though the look of amusement hadn't left his eyes. "Good day, Miss Lambert."

"Good day, Archie," she said, with one final look behind her at Valentine. His eyes, however, were not amused — they were smoldering. And she was well aware why.

* * *

THE PASSAGEWAY between the long gallery and Valentine's bedroom was well utilized over the next two weeks. Valentine hadn't wanted Rebecca to feel obligated to come to him again, but when she appeared in his dressing room the night after their first liaison, he certainly hadn't been disappointed.

She was everything he could have asked for in a woman. She was a beauty, to be sure, but it was more than that. She cared for others more than she did herself. She certainly looked after her father, who was so scattered it was difficult to imagine how he had come up with such intricate, impressive designs. For it was not only his creativity that impressed Valentine, but also that the modern conveniences and the practicalities he incorporated seemed so innovative. It was hard to reconcile them with the man who often seemed to think he was elsewhere and spent most of his time reminiscing about the past.

In fact, it seemed like a foolish thing to even consider, but the designs reminded him somewhat of... well, of Rebecca. Practical yet with an appreciation for the aesthetic. Striking yet simple. He was about to say as much to her but then thought he would sound like the uncultured man he was, so he let it pass.

But as they gathered around the dining room, where Mr. Lambert and Rebecca had laid out his plans, he was reminded of his thoughts again. While he should have been focused on her father, Valentine couldn't help that his gaze continued to wander over toward Rebecca, who sat across from him in a deep-green gown that brought out the highlights in her eyes.

Mr. Lambert had just finished explaining how he had tied in the various styles of the house from over the years with his current neoclassical style, and was now reviewing the additional wing he would add to the estate. Rebecca then chimed in, pointing out the innovations her father had added — a shower off of Valentine's bedchamber, moving some of the servant's areas so that they would be closer to the rooms they served.

"I love it," Mrs. St. Vincent said with a wide grin, and Valentine nodded, though he was not quite as thrilled as his mother was. It was masterly, to be sure, but there was no way to pay for any of this without sending the dukedom even deeper into debt. His mother didn't seem to care, but then, why would she? It was not her responsibility to look after his properties nor his finances.

He scratched his head, trying to find the best way to put into words what he needed to say without Mr. Lambert thinking he was being insulting.

"It is very fine work, Mr. Lambert," he said. "I am much impressed."

Rebecca eyed him, raising an eyebrow. He knew her expressions well enough now to know she was asking him what the "but" was.

"I am simply unsure if we need it all to be quite *so* impressive," he said. "Such as the additional wing. We don't even use all of the rooms we currently have."

Mr. Lambert stood, pushing back his chair, a frown twisting the corners of his lips.

"You said you wanted an extra wing! It was no small feat to design."

"I understand, Mr. Lambert, and no matter what we do, I will pay you for your time. It is just that—"

"Of all the rudeness. Just what I would expect of an upstart like you!"

Rebecca gasped at her father's words, and Valentine slowly rose to his feet.

"Mr. Lambert," he said, breathing slowly as he worked to keep his temper in check, for Rebecca's sake more than any other reason. "I believe that was uncalled for."

"I'm sure you didn't mean that, Father," Rebecca said, rounding the table to stand between the two men. "We apologize, Val— your grace."

"Rebecca, that is enough. You will not speak for me in this," Mr. Lambert said, stepping forward so that she was behind him once more. "I—"

"Good afternoon!"

Jemima stepped into the dining room, and Valentine breathed a sigh of relief. For once in her life, his sister had impeccable timing. Her hair was slightly askew, but she was distracted enough that she did not immediately pick up on the animosity in the room, as her attention was caught by the house plans on the table.

"Oh, your plans are finished, how lovely!"

She bent over them and began running her finger along some of the rooms, reading the descriptions of each. "How smart," she murmured as she reviewed them. "Oh, and you have created a laboratory for me in this estate as well! Thank you, Mr. Lambert. I so appreciate it."

Except, why, Valentine wondered, was she looking at Rebecca?

"We did think you would enjoy it," Rebecca said before her father could open his mouth again. "Now, come, Father, why do we not return to the gallery for a while and discuss things a little further?"

She gathered the plans in her arms.

"We shall see you all at dinner. Good afternoon."

Her father looked as though he wanted to say something more, but at Rebecca's pointed gaze, he sighed in defeat and followed after her.

The St. Vincents simply stared at one another afterward, and Val wondered just what was going on.

CHAPTER 17

*R*ebecca was cleaning up her papers and pencils from the revisions she had completed following the disaster of a meeting they had held when Jemima entered the room. Her strawberry-blonde hair was pulled back tightly away from her face, though small ringlets had escaped, held back by a headband she had fashioned.

"Am I disturbing you?" she asked as she paused in the doorway, a questioning look on her face.

"Not at all," Rebecca said, looking up with a smile. "In fact, I am pleased to see you." The two of them had become much closer over the past couple of weeks. Jemima had a sharp mind, one that was constantly working, solving problems and determining more ingenuities.

Jemima took a seat on the wooden chair where Rebecca's father purportedly worked and leaned an elbow back on his desk.

"You've been busy," she remarked, and Rebecca nodded.

"Yes, helping my father," she said. "He has been making some revisions following our meeting with your brother earlier today. He was thinking that if we do not add another wing, as was the original plan, then we could—"

"Rebecca," Jemima gently interrupted. "Your father does not care that Valentine has no money to pay for these renovations, as long as he is getting paid."

"Oh, but of course he does. Or, at least, he will design everything to Valentine's specifications. He—"

Warmth crept into her cheeks when she realized that she had used Valentine's given name.

"That is to say—"

But she stopped at Jemima's knowing expression. At first she thought Val's sister had guessed at her relationship with Valentine, but then she completely surprised her.

"Rebecca, I know that it is not your father who has drawn all of these plans."

"Wh-what do you mean?" Rebecca managed.

Jemima rose and walked over to study the drawings once more.

"Look at these," she said. "The innovation, the care you've taken. You have thought of everything. There is a laboratory for me, a sitting room for mother, a training room for Val. Your father may be an incredible architect in his own right, but his focus would be on creating a legacy for himself and his own name. He would be looking to add a ballroom that would be talked about by all who attend. A library that stretches to the sky with angels circling the ceiling and raining down books. But that is not what these plans hold. You have turned this very room into a library, because it makes sense. We do not have the paintings to create another long gallery, but I'm sure we can find books enough to fill it."

Rebecca was speechless, and Jemima just smiled.

"I am more observant than you might think. One has to be, as a scientist. The most interesting experiments are not those that you control, but those that are taking place in the chaos of the world around you."

Rebecca sat heavily in her own chair, her gaze remaining on Jemima.

"I did everything I could just to help my father at first," she said, hoping that if she explained herself well enough, Jemima would forgive her deception. "But when he began to lose interest in his work, I took it up myself because, truth be told, we needed the money after he took part in a foolish project."

"But your father is losing his mental capacity, isn't he?" Jemima said with a sympathetic gaze, and Rebecca nodded, a lump forming in her throat that she could finally unburden herself, share her deepest secrets with someone who might partially understand.

"It's getting worse," she said, her words gutted. "And I don't know what to do about it."

"Have you told Val?" Jemima asked, and Rebecca shook her head furiously.

"No. And please, promise you will not say anything."

"Are you worried that he will fire you?" Jemima asked, tilting her head and studying Rebecca. "I do not think he would, for he appreciates what you have done so far, and he is clearly not the type of man to begrudge a woman's intellect. You— oooh," she said, bringing a hand to her chin.

Rebecca's eyes widened. What secret had Jemima apparently stumbled upon now?

"You love him," Jemima stated.

"I do not *love* him," Rebecca said with a gasp, and Jemima's eyebrows shot up nearly as high as her forehead at the emphasis of Rebecca's words.

"That is to say, I—"

"You care for him, then," Jemima stated, and when Rebecca opened her mouth to protest, Jemima shook her head. "I have been an idiot," she murmured. "Now that I think on it, it was there all along. Oh, I wish you had told me."

Rebecca looked down at her hands, somewhat ashamed.

"You are his sister," she said awkwardly, and Jemima nodded.

"I am," she said, rising and coming over toward Rebecca, taking her hands in hers. "And I approve wholeheartedly."

"You would likely be the only one," Rebecca said softly, willing the tears to retreat back into her eyes. "I am not the woman for him, Jemima. I have no title, no prospects, and no money, particularly if my plan doesn't work."

"And what plan is that?"

Rebecca, relieved of the change in subject from her affections for Valentine, quickly described for Jemima their current crisis with the speculative housing, and her idea to hold a lottery with the prizes being the houses themselves.

"It should catch interest," she mused, "though my father fears that the neighbors will not be particularly pleased that just anyone might find themselves the owner of such a home."

"That is no one's problem but their own," said Jemima with a sniff, and Rebecca realized that she had basically been describing the St. Vincent's own rise in fortunes.

"Yes, well, we may have to receive permission from the Crown to move forward, and I worry that we will never do so," Rebecca said, and Jemima nodded knowingly.

"Have you asked Valentine to help?"

"No," Rebecca said, shaking her head. "And I have no plan to. He has more than enough to worry about without my own troubles."

"Jemima!" Her mother's voice carried down the hall and Jemima sighed, rolling her eyes at Rebecca.

"I best go. Mama wants to invite one of the neighbors

over tomorrow, and she insists that I add my name to the invitation. But please, Rebecca, give Valentine a chance. Tell him the truth of it all. You never know what good could come of it."

"I will," Rebecca promised. "I'm not sure when, but I will."

"Good," Jemima said with a teasing grin, "because I am terrible at keeping secrets."

"Jemima!" Rebecca laughed as her friend left the room.

She took a seat with a sigh. She was terribly relieved to have someone to share the truth with, although now she was fretting about speaking with Valentine. He had told her a few times now that one of the qualities he most admired about her was her straightforwardness, her willingness to always be there to support others.

But she had been selfish. She designed in part to help her father and maintain his legacy, true, but there was more to it. She worked because she loved it. Taking a pencil to paper and letting her ideas run free through her drawings brought her more joy than nearly anything else, and she didn't want to let it go.

If Valentine — or his mother — ever named her as a fraud, then she would never work again. Nor would her father. They would lose everything — his good name, their work, any future income, and her ability to do what she loved.

Yet the closer they grew, the more apparent it was that she needed to tell him, and she would.

She just had to find the right time.

* * *

"Mr. Lambert, I am pleased that we could reconvene," Valentine said as he and the architect sat across from one another in the drawing room. "I am sure we can come to an understanding."

The truth of it was that if anyone had insulted him so in his former life he would not likely have been quite as determined to find a resolution. But this was Rebecca's father, for one, and a respected architect, for another.

So he would be polite, civil, and work through this.

"I'm sure we can," Mr. Lambert said, though his gaze was off in the distance.

Valentine opened his mouth to continue, but just then, there was a knock at the door.

"Come in," Valentine called, expecting a footman with a drink for the two of them.

But it was Rebecca, looking as splendid as always. She held out house plans toward them, then began to explain.

"Father, you forgot these in the long gallery. These are the revisions you made following your previous discussion with his grace."

Mr. Lambert looked at her oddly.

"I do not recall making such revisions."

"Oh, Father, don't be silly," she said, a desperate expression on her face. "Of course you did. Here you are, your grace."

She passed him the drawings, but didn't leave the room. Valentine unfurled them and began to study them, delight leaping into his countenance at what he would say. The complex had been made simple, the grandeur elegant now instead of what would be, in his mind, quite expensive.

"This is perfect," he said, a smile growing on his face as he looked between father and daughter. "Mr. Lambert, these are—"

"Rubbish!" Lambert said, and Valentine's head tilted up.

"Pardon me?"

"What we did before was much better. These are rubbish.

But," he threw his hands in the air, "if this is what you want, then so be it."

He sighed as Valentine stared at him and then at the plans. Something wasn't right. It just didn't add up. There was no way that Mr. Lambert had—

But then he lost his sequence of thought when his mother appeared in the doorway.

"Valentine!" she said, her face wreathed in smiles and his stomach became rather queasy. Those were the smiles she usually wore when they were out in polite society — when she was trying to prove herself as mother to a duke, despite her rather common beginnings.

"I have a surprise!" she said. "Lady Rothwell is here to visit. They are but a short ride away. And she has brought her daughter, Lady Fredericka. Jemima will be joining us in a moment, but I thought perhaps that you and I could entertain them until she arrives?"

Valentine rose, furious with his mother for not providing him with any warning of such a visit. But then the woman and her daughter entered, and he had no choice but to nod in greeting and be as polite as was expected of a man of his station.

"Good morning," he mumbled, stealing a look over at Rebecca. Her eyes had widened and the corners of her lips had dropped. What was the matter with her?

He followed her eyes to Lady Fredericka. She was a pretty thing. Quite tiny, with brown hair piled high on her head, her eyes a warm brown. She did seem friendly, at least. Then he looked over at his mother, who was smiling as though she had been named Queen of England. Lady Rothwell's expression was near matching.

And then he realized what this was about, and what had so dismayed Rebecca.

His mother was making a match for him.

"Lady Rothwell, Lady Fredericka," he finally managed. "This is our architect, Mr. Lambert, and his daughter, Miss Lambert. They are staying with us—"

"To complete my father's work, but he is now finished," Rebecca said, clearly choosing to ignore the open-mouth stares of the women at the fact she would interrupt a duke, but she needed away from this room as quickly as possible. "We will be returning to London tomorrow."

"Re— Miss Lambert," he said with a silent warning as it felt as though he had been punched in the stomach, "perhaps we should speak of this later?"

"Yes, let us do that," Mrs. St. Vincent said, clapping her hands together. "Would you mind excusing us, Mr. Lambert, Miss Lambert?"

"Of course," Rebecca said, gathering her father's things, though Valentine didn't miss the silent anger and dismay emanating from her. "Good day. It was a pleasure to meet you both."

And as she sailed to the door, Valentine was powerless to do anything but watch her go.

CHAPTER 18

*R*ebecca rushed around the long gallery, furiously blinking away the tears that threatened to fall. She refused to allow them. She had known what the outcome of this brief interlude with Valentine would be. He had to marry a woman of his own class now. A woman who would integrate him within the nobility, who would have a dowry that could restore the dukedom to its former glory.

The only role she played within that scenario was ensuring that his homes were befitting of the Duke of Wyndham and would properly impress all who visited.

She had placed all of her tools in a large bag and was half-dragging, half-carrying it out of the room to leave it by the entrance when she stumbled into someone. She just about went flying backward when a hand came out to steady her.

"I say, are you all right, Miss Lambert?"

Rebecca looked up to see a warm smile from underneath questioning brown eyes.

"Lady Fredericka," she said, righting herself. "My apologies. I was just—"

"Leaving?" the woman asked, and Rebecca couldn't help

but appreciate the beautiful gown she wore. It was cream with a lace fichu, red ribboning around the hem and neckline.

"Soon," Rebecca said with a nod, eager to be away from the woman who may take on the role she had come to realize she very, very much would have aspired to assume herself — that of Valentine's wife.

"Are you all right, Miss Lambert?" Lady Fredericka asked, peering up at Rebecca, for despite the fact that Rebecca wasn't overly tall, this woman was quite short. Valentine would tower over top of her.

"I'm fine," Rebecca said hurriedly. "Can I help you with anything?"

"Oh, no," the woman said, shaking her head. "I just needed a moment alone in the powder room." She blushed. "I suppose I shouldn't admit such a thing."

Rebecca couldn't help but laugh. "If there is anyone that is comfortable in speaking of such things, it would be me."

"I'm pleased to hear it," Lady Fredericka said and then sighed. "Well, I am sorry that you are leaving. You seem quite lovely, and I could use a friend or two close by. Perhaps if we are both ever in London we could take tea together."

Rebecca couldn't hide her shock. "With me? Lady Fredericka, I am flattered, but I am simply the daughter of an architect, and you are—"

"Freddie," she finished. "Call me Freddie. I much prefer it. Well, good day, Miss Lambert. I hope to see you again."

Rebecca could only stare after her as she quickly and efficiently strode down the hall with her short strides.

Damn it. She liked her.

* * *

REBECCA DIDN'T COME to him that night.

Valentine waited, quite impatiently, but she never showed up through his dressing room door. He took the stairs down to the long gallery himself, but when he arrived, it was completely empty of both her and any sign that she or her father had ever been there. The fire had even simmered to embers. It was as it had been before they had arrived. The thought filled him with such melancholy that he had to leave the room.

And try to determine just where her bedchamber was located.

He was like a prowler in his own home as he strode down the corridor of the guest wing. He had to be careful — her father had likely been placed in a room quite close. This was ridiculous, he reasoned as he stopped in front of one door after another, listening for sounds within. He was a duke for goodness sake, and this was his estate. He shouldn't feel the thief.

And yet he was. He had stolen from Rebecca her innocence, despite the fact she had freely given it, and he felt the very bounder that he was. He was the son of a physician who hadn't been good enough to follow in his father's footsteps, so instead he had relied on his baser urges and become a pugilist. His decision had led to the loss of his brother. The fact that he was a duke now? Dumb luck, more than anything.

He was about to give up and return to his own bedroom when one of the doors opened a crack and a beautiful dark head emerged.

"Val?"

"Rebecca!" he exhaled, quickly crossing toward her. He was ready to take her in his arms but he stopped short. Would she reject him?

"May I come in?"

"Of course," she said, opening the door wider, though she

stepped back and crossed her arms over her chest, barring herself from him.

He closed the door gently behind him, looking around at the room she had inhabited during her stay here. The heavy curtains were pulled over the windows, leaving the room in near darkness aside from light from the fire in the grate and the lone candle that burned beside her bed.

"Where were you going?" he asked.

"Pardon me?"

"You opened the door."

"Oh," she said, the smallest of smiles licking at her lips. "I heard you in the hall. You were bumbling about with the grace of a brawler instead of the fine pugilist you are."

He snorted. "I would hardly think you would have ascertained that from the fight you saw." He sat heavily in the armchair near the window. "I am actually much better than that, you know."

"I don't doubt it," she said, sitting on the edge of the bed. She wore a night-rail that was as elegant as she was. It lacked lace frippery or ruffles or any other adornment but allowed her true beauty to emerge.

Val leaned forward, his elbows on his knees.

"You didn't come to me tonight."

"I couldn't," she said, her teeth raking over her plush bottom lip.

"Why not?" he asked, the air still and tense as he waited for her answer.

"Because, Val," she said, walking over to him, kneeling in front of him and placing her hands over his. She looked up at him and he nearly forgot himself in the forest of her eyes under her thick lashes. "Today was a reminder that you are not mine. You never will be. We have to stop this charade, for the more we are together, the more it will hurt when we must be separated."

"I have no wish to be separated from you," he said, his voice rough to his own ears. He was not a man used to expressing such emotion, and the words were foreign on his lips.

"That may be so," she said with a sad smile, "but being with me would do nothing for you."

"It could," he said, hope and excitement spurring his heart to beat faster as he thought of it. "Perhaps, we could make it work, you and I."

"What of the dowry you are seeking? The respectability?"

He shrugged, at a loss. He hadn't thought it through, but the urge to be with her was overwhelming all reason.

"So we dispense with the renovations for now. We'll keep your father's plans, put them into place someday. You could be my duchess, Rebecca, and we will learn the life together."

"We would never be accepted by the *ton*."

They wouldn't — not really. Oh, they would be welcomed, but ridiculed. He didn't want that for Rebecca, and yet he couldn't promise her much else. He thought of his father, what he would have said about him shuffling away his ducal responsibility for the woman he wanted in his bed, in his life. Valentine had always done what was best for him and no one else. Because of that, Matthew was dead. Now, what of his mother? What of Jemima? He ran a hand over his face, which Rebecca reached up and caught within hers.

"Tomorrow, my father and I will return to London," she said. "There is work we need to complete, and he will start on the renovations to your London house. By the time you return, it will be livable. Perhaps, after some separation, we will know better what we both want."

He didn't want her to go, but he had no reason for keeping her with him any longer. He would return with her, but he needed to interview stewards first and put his affairs here in order.

"I will return as soon as I am able," he promised, clutching her hand to his chest.

She nodded, her eyes shimmering in the dim light. He reached down and picked her up effortlessly, bringing her to sit on his lap as he held her close, wishing he could capture this moment as more than a memory, keeping her with him forever. He buried his nose in her hair, inhaling the scent of rose petals that had become so familiar.

Her hands came around his neck as she held him with the same strength. Valentine had no idea how long they sat there like that, no words required as they simply held one another as close as could be.

"Rebecca…" he began, needing to share with her all. They had been as close as could be physically, but she deserved more from him.

"You know that I never wanted this title."

"I do."

"And you know it should have been my brother's, but… he died."

"I know, and I'm sorry Valentine."

Valentine paused. "It's more than that. He's dead because of me."

Rebecca was silent, but the trust in her hazel green eyes was nearly more than he could bear.

"I'm sure that isn't true," she said quietly.

"I wish that were so," he responded, hearing the heaviness in his voice as he began telling the story that had been replaying in his mind for the past few years. "We had come to London — this was before we knew my cousin had been deemed illegitimate. I agreed to a prizefight, one against a new young lord, a member of the Fancy who wanted to prove himself. I beat him — soundly. He was humiliated, as he had reason to be, but there was no way I was letting him win just because of who he was."

He stopped, this part nearly too hard to put into words.

"He sent a group of men upon me the next night, to teach me a lesson. They found where I was staying, saw me leaving the house, and attacked." He swallowed hard. "Only, it wasn't me. It was Matthew. We always looked a good deal alike, but especially in the dark, they didn't see the truth. He— he died from his injuries."

"Oh, Valentine," Rebecca said, sorrow in her voice, and he could only nod jerkily.

"The worst of it is that the young lord was killed in another prizefight he should never have entered before I could do anything about it."

"None of this was your fault," she said gently.

"It is," he insisted. "If I hadn't fought—"

"But you had fought plenty of times before, I'm sure. It was the fault of the nobleman, not of you at all."

"It should have been me who died."

She jerked back. "Don't say such a thing!"

"But it should have. My parents never recovered. My father died soon after, likely of a broken heart. He had never approved of me to begin with but after that... anyway. It is why I do what I can now, to try to support my family as best I can."

"That is admirable, Valentine, but I still believe you are far too hard on yourself."

"So be it."

Finally, she leaned back, but only far enough that she could press her lips against his. He accepted her kiss eagerly, like a thirsty man desperate for a drink of water. He picked her up and carried her over to the bed, laying her down as though she were fine china.

They had made love in many ways before — passionately, languidly, with a fair bit of fun and laughter. But this time was different.

This time when they came together, there was a sense of melancholy about their joining. They kissed one another as though it was the last time they would ever do so, savoring the moments, the touches, the caresses.

When they came together, it was as wonderful as it always was, but a heavy weight filled Val's heart with the innate knowledge that this was farewell, in one way or another.

It was just left to determine how permanent that farewell might be.

* * *

JEMIMA WOULDN'T STOP STARING at him the next morning across the breakfast table.

"What?" Valentine asked around his mouthful of food.

"Are you all right?" she asked, peering at him carefully.

"Of course I am!" he said, though he realized he may have been slightly too emphatic, for she narrowed her eyes at him. "Why wouldn't I be?"

"Because Rebecca has left."

Thankfully their mother had yet to join them at the breakfast table.

"Why should it matter that Miss Lambert has returned to London? Besides the fact that we had to lend her and her father one of the carriages that is in a sorry state of repair. I do hope it makes it to London."

"You know why it matters, Valentine."

His sister was far too smart.

"I don't know what you are talking about," he lied, refusing to capitulate. "We will also be in London soon enough ourselves."

"Yes, I am looking forward to it," Jemima said. "I have much to discuss with Celeste, and I, for one, am not ashamed to admit that I rather liked Rebecca and I look forward to seeing her again. I am sure she and Celeste would get along famously. Are you looking forward to taking your seat in the House of Lords?"

"No."

She laughed. "I didn't think so. But think of all the good you can do, coming with a different perspective than the rest of them."

"I suppose."

"My, you are sullen this morning," she said, tilting her head, goading him.

"Must you be so contrary?" he muttered.

"Yes, until you admit the truth," she said. "Now tell me, what did you think of Lady Fredericka?"

He shrugged. The truth was, he hadn't given her much thought, for his mind was too filled with Rebecca.

"She seems like a nice young lady."

"She is," Jemima said, her eyes lighting up. "She and I got along famously. She is quite intelligent, speaks of much beyond the silly nothings most women talk about, and I found her quite kind. I wouldn't say, however, that the two of you seemed overly interested in one another. In fact, you hardly said a word to her."

"I have other things on my mind."

"Like Rebecca."

He glared at her. "No, like getting this estate in order. I have interviews today with five men who may be good candidates to become steward here, and when I return to London, I must find a competent man-of-business. I need someone I can trust."

"You trust Archie."

"Yes, but Archie has not the connections nor the knowledge to put this estate in order," he said. "I need someone with ideas that are outside of the usual."

"Like Rebecca's scheme."

"What are you talking about?" he asked, attempting not to show how intrigued he was by Jemima's words, but regardless needing to know more.

Jemima quickly told him of Rebecca's father's failed project and her idea of how to earn back the money they needed.

"A lottery with the houses as the prizes themselves," he murmured. "Interesting."

Jemima nodded as she picked up her coffee cup, taking a sip. "Very. She is quite intelligent."

"So she is," Valentine admitted. Much more than he, that was for certain.

Archie appeared in the doorway with a nod, telling Valentine that he must prepare for his first interview. Val knew it was quite unusual for a valet to sit in, but he needed someone he trusted to provide a second opinion, and at the moment, Archie was the best person to fit that role.

"Well, good day, Jem. Best wishes on whatever it is you are embarking on today."

"Thank you, Val," she said with a wink. "To you as well."

One thing was for certain — he had to keep an eye on his sister. She was too smart for her own good.

CHAPTER 19

*R*ebecca was typically one who found the positives in life. She prided herself on making the best of even the most tragic of situations. She and her father had turned the most ghastly of buildings into the incredible. She enjoyed her life despite the fact that she hadn't had any prospects nor even much opportunity to find a man who might consider her as a bride.

Most men she was acquainted with were noble, or colleagues of her father's who were typically far older than she. None of the noblemen, of course, saw her as anything more than a woman to be trifled with, so she had avoided any liaisons. Until now.

Now she was hopelessly falling for a man who would never truly be hers — except for that fact that he held her heart and likely always would.

She might have been able to handle that if it wasn't for the fact that she was reading about him in the society papers. He was returning to London, the papers read, and there he would find himself a wife. The most likely candidate, according to the talk, was Lady Fredericka Ashworth, with whom he had been spending a great deal of time at his country estate near Hungerford.

The worst part was that Rebecca knew the woman would likely make a good bride for Valentine, and she could never begrudge him the match, for Lady Fredericka — Freddie, she reminded herself — seemed to be an amiable woman who would make a lovely life companion.

Rebecca groaned as she and her father climbed the steps of Valentine's London home once more. And now she had to be reminded of her feelings for the man every day they arrived here, as the renovations were to begin.

The truth was that they weren't so much renovations as *completions* and they would not take overly long.

And then there was the housing speculation. They had been hit by one obstruction after another. The only way Rebecca saw her lottery plan working now was through Crown approval — or divine intervention, which, at this point, seemed more likely.

They were greeted by the butler, Dexter, as they had been upon their first arrival. Rebecca reminisced about the initial meeting between her and Valentine. It seemed like so long ago now, though, in reality, it was only just a couple of months ago. So very much had changed in such a short time.

They had been strangers then, when she had first seen him half-clothed in his dressing room. Now she knew him so much better. She knew every sculpted line of his body. As for his heart — well, she thought she knew that much better as well, though there was so much more to discover.

"Lovely to see you again, Dexter," Rebecca said in greeting now as Val's London butler opened the door to her.

"And you, Miss Lambert, Mr. Lambert," he said, taking their cloaks. "Did you enjoy Stonehall?"

"We did, thank you," Rebecca said.

"Hungerford turns rather chilly at this time of year," he remarked, and Rebecca turned to him with some interest.

"It does," she agreed. "You have been there before?"

"Of course, Miss Lambert," he said with a boyish grin. "It's where I'm from. Where we're all from, actually. We knew Val — his grace before he became duke, and he only hires those he trusts. Which means he must think highly of you."

How interesting, Rebecca thought as they made their way through the house. First Archie, and now Dexter. Men who were not necessarily trained in their actual positions, but knew more about Valentine than any others would.

She and her father were to meet today with the builder and discuss the forthcoming plans. They had received a missive from Mrs. St. Vincent, however, with one instruction — the ballroom was to be ready by the time the Season began in earnest, for they would be hosting a ball with all of London's finest to be invited.

They were to set up in the parlor, but Rebecca heard voices coming from the drawing room as they passed. Eager to see Jemima, she forgot her place for a moment as she paused in the doorway.

"Jem—"

The words died on her lips as she saw who Jemima was conversing with. Lady Fredericka.

"My apologies," she murmured, embarrassed. "I didn't mean to interrupt."

"Oh, no, do come in," Jemima said, rising and walking to the door with a true smile on her face. "I am so happy to see you, Rebecca. Please join us."

"Oh, no, I should—"

"Please?" Jemima said, raising her eyebrows, and Rebecca didn't have it within her to say no. When she walked into the drawing room she saw that in actuality it was not just Jemima and Lady Fredericka present, but there was a third woman in the room. She had a shock of red hair, her nose was covered in freckles, and a warm smile crossed her face when she saw Rebecca.

"Rebecca, this is Celeste Keswick, a good friend of mine," she introduced her, and the woman began to rise from the chair, though her foot got caught in the arm as it had been folded underneath her.

"Forgive me," she said as she slightly stumbled while walking toward Rebecca. "It is nice to meet you. Jem has told us much about you."

"Oh," Rebecca said, stealing a look over at Jemima, wondering just how much she had shared. Her heart quickened ever so slightly as she wondered if she had shared *everything*, particularly with Lady Fredericka who just might become Valentine's bride.

Jemima shook her head just slightly, enough to tell Rebecca that she hadn't shared *all* her secrets.

"You are an astronomer," she said to Miss Keswick as she took a seat, remembering Jemima telling her about her friend.

"Lovely of you to say so," Miss Keswick said with a laugh. "I do enjoy looking at the stars. Call me Celeste, please."

"She is being modest," Jemima said, reaching toward the table between them and pouring Rebecca a cup of tea. "She is hoping to make the next great discovery."

Celeste's cheeks turned a shade of cherry red, and Rebecca guessed the woman had the misfortune to blush easily.

"Well, I wish you the best of luck," Rebecca said, meaning each word.

"We are discovering that Lady Fredericka—"

"Freddie," she cut in.

"*Freddie* is a kindred soul as well," Jemima said, smiling at the small woman. "She *invents* things."

"You do?" Rebecca said, turning toward Freddie. "What types of things?"

Freddie shrugged, her lips turning in a small smile. "Nothing of note, really. A few things to help women that men would never think to invent, I suppose. If you observe others long enough, you see where some things might be useful."

"She devised a way to cook eggs using the steam of a kettle," Jemima said, and Rebecca's jaw dropped slightly.

"That is impressive," she said. "How does it work?"

Soon enough, Rebecca found herself in deep conversation with the woman she had been trying to avoid. Her mind whirled with possibilities.

"And then there is the bed which allows for exercise."

"Truly?" she said, intrigued. "Well, perhaps we can incorporate such a bed into this house," she said, leaning back with a satisfied grin. "We shall have to talk to Valentine."

The reminder of him slightly deflated the bubble of enthusiasm that had surrounded her, but she refused to give into it.

Freddie tilted her head and studied Rebecca for a moment. "You know quite a bit about house design. I suppose it makes sense, having lived and worked with your father for so long."

"Exactly," Rebecca murmured, taking a sip of her tea as she realized she had revealed far more than she had ever meant to.

"In what capacity do you assist him?" Freddie asked, sipping her tea herself, though her eyes were shrewd as she watched Rebecca carefully while she answered the question.

"I, ah, I'm his secretary," Rebecca said, setting down her teacup.

"Well, even in such work, you must come to understand all that he does," Freddie said with a smile, though Rebecca could read the glint in her brown eyes, telling her that Freddie was just as aware as Jemima that Rebecca was likely far more than a secretary. It seemed a woman who worked unconventionally herself could see beyond what most others did to find a similar soul. Somehow, however, Rebecca sensed that Freddie would keep her secret, and she gave her the slightest nod of thanks.

"I'd best be going," Rebecca said, hoping her father had remembered why he was here — to meet with the master builder. "It was lovely to meet you, Miss Keswick."

"Celeste."

"And to see you again, Jemima, Freddie."

They murmured their farewells, and Rebecca exited with some regret. How she wished she could stay and share all with them, to have others she could confide in — others who understood her longing to do what made her happy and to be recognized for it.

The thought wouldn't leave her as she sat down next to her father in the parlor, where he and the master-builder were discussing good times from the past. Thank goodness, Rebecca thought with relief, for that was one subject her father was still well-versed in. She looked over the plans now in front of them — plans that she had painstakingly drawn with her own hand.

Those were her balusters lining the staircase, so intricate in detail that one could see the floral design on each one. That was her clever integration of Jemima's laboratory in the conservatory, which would be constructed so that it was easily hidden when necessary, great chemistry lurking behind the citrus plants and bougainvillea.

But it would all be attributed to her father.

And then, just when she thought her despair couldn't pitch to any lower depths, Valentine walked into the room. Their eyes caught, held, so many words between them unsaid and yet understood. They had been separated for long enough that Rebecca had nearly convinced herself that she didn't need him any longer — nearly. For the truth was as obvious as the broken nose on his face. She yearned to throw herself in his arms, despite the presence of any others in the room, and tell him how much she had missed him, how she longed to be with him once more.

Instead, she simply smiled demurely and greeted him with, "Your grace."

He nodded at her, though he broke convention and bowed before her, taking her hand in his and murmuring, "Miss Lambert," as he brought her hand up to his lips for a quick kiss.

Even Rebecca's father noticed the motion, and he was typically oblivious to anything and everything around him that did not pertain to houses, estates, or public buildings.

Conversation halted for a moment until Valentine began to speak. He may not have been a duke for long, but he was still a duke, and these men knew enough to understand that when a man who was not only a duke but an employer directed them, they must continue with what they were paid to do — despite Rebecca's father's pride, which continued to blockade them.

"It is good to see you again, Mr. Lambert," Valentine said. "And you must be Mr. Burton. You come with the highest of recommendations."

"Thank you, your grace," the builder said. "I do hope I live up to them."

"You'd best," Valentine said, with the unspoken promise that if he didn't, he would find another.

Trust was not easily won with Valentine.

"Mr. Lambert!" Mrs. St. Vincent sailed into the room, her cloying perfume announcing her presence before she entered. "I am so glad you are here. And you must be the builder. There is much urgency."

"Oh?" Rebecca couldn't help but ask.

"I see you are also here once more, Miss Lambert," Valentine's mother said, and Rebecca didn't miss the disdain in her voice. Interesting. It had never been there before, in all the time they had spent together. "But yes. You see, we will be hosting a ball in a month's time."

"That is far too soon!" Rebecca protested, but that only earned her one of Mrs. St. Vincent's expressions of ire.

"It doesn't all have to be completed. Just enough of the ballroom that it is impressive enough for visitors. It is nearly there already. Isn't that right, Valentine?"

He said nothing but looked extremely uncomfortable.

"The ball is most important," she continued. "Valentine has yet to find a bride, and it is becoming rather imperative he does so."

Rebecca's stomach twisted in a knot.

"Is it possible?"

Rebecca's father and Mr. Burton shared a look, and Mr. Burton nodded.

"Not all the fine detail and the painting, of course," he said. "But as we are simply completing it and not starting from the beginning, then I'm sure it is possible for us to have it finished enough for you to host your ball."

"Very good," Mrs. St. Vincent said, clapping her hands.

Valentine looked as though he wanted to punch someone.

Rebecca only wished she could do the same.

CHAPTER 20

*V*alentine had excused himself as quickly as was possible and then had decided to lie in wait.

He wasn't very good at waiting. He had situated himself in the as yet unfinished but comfortably furnished drawing room, recently vacated by his sister and her friends. He was glad that Jemima had gotten on well with Lady Fredericka — at least one of them had developed a relationship with her.

Finally — *finally* — he saw a flash of green fabric, and he sprinted out the door with all of the speed required of a pugilist.

"Rebecca!"

She swirled around so fast that a couple of pins fell out of her hair and pieces of her midnight tresses cascaded around her shoulders.

She was alone. Thank God.

They paused in the hall for a moment, staring at one another from across the corridor.

Then, without breaking the connection held between their shared gazes, they began to move toward one another — slowly at first, but their footsteps soon quickened, and before Valentine knew it, she had launched herself into his arms, or maybe he had scooped her up and thrown her in the air, he wasn't entirely sure.

All he knew that when their lips met, it was as though all that he had been worried about over the past couple of weeks without her simply disappeared.

He had no idea how long they stood there in the corridor with their arms entwined around one another, but voices from down the hall soon had him stepping back into the drawing room, though he didn't let her go.

Finally, he set her down and they just stood there, her cool hands upon his face, stroking, exploring.

Until they stopped.

"You fought again."

"I—" The lie began to form, but he couldn't keep the truth from her. She was too important for that.

"I did," he admitted. "But not to worry. I won this time."

She dropped her hands along with her chin.

"I still worry."

"It's over now."

"This fight is," she said with the slightest of bitterness in her tone.

"Yes."

"You weren't hurt this time?" she asked quietly.

"I was not."

He wouldn't apologize for fighting. He had to do so — he had these renovations to pay for, in addition to ensuring the dukedom didn't go further into debt.

"How is everything else?" she asked, her gaze returning to his, her eyes searching.

"I think it's improving," he said, leaving her now and walking over to the sideboard, ignoring the tea sitting out on the table and pouring himself a stiff drink instead. "I've found a steward for Stonehall who I hope I can trust."

"Do you know him?"

He snapped his gaze to her.

"I do. He's a friend of Archie's." He took a sip of his drink. "How did you know?"

"You seem to enjoy going back to the familiar."

He reflected on her words. He hadn't really thought of it like that. He swirled the amber liquid around in his drink.

"I like knowing what to expect," he finally said. "And it's important to be able to trust those around me."

Valentine couldn't be sure, but it seemed a flicker of panic crossed Rebecca's face, though only for a moment.

"I do hope it works out for you," she said instead, trailing her fingertips along the back of the chesterfield that looked horribly out of place in the room. "Do you think those who worked for the former duke were stealing from your estate?"

He had reflected upon that question for quite some time, though actually determining the fact through the ledgers had proven a little more difficult as they had been so lazy there were missing accounts.

"The best I can tell is that it was mismanagement," he said with a shrug, though he didn't tell her that it was actually Jemima who had determined that and not him. "People being lazy, not being held accountable."

"Will you hire a man of business?"

"I will," he said. "But—"

"It's a matter of finding someone you can trust," she finished for him, and he nodded with a half-grin. She was coming to know him well.

Now that he had overcome the joy — for it was joy, there was no other way to describe the shafts of sunbeams that had coursed through him — upon seeing her, he took a closer look at her. Slight dark circles were apparent underneath her eyes, and her skin was rather pale.

"Are you all right?" he asked, drawing closer, and she nodded, though her response was rather too quick.

"Of course," she said. "Why wouldn't I be?"

"You look... tired," he finally settled upon and she drew up tall.

"A woman never wants to be told she looks *tired*, Val," she admonished him. "It is basically saying that I look awful."

"You could never look awful," he said, attempting to save himself. "Just unwell."

That, at least, brought sparks back into her eyes.

"You would tell me if anything is the matter?" he asked.

But while she responded with a terse, "Of course," she looked away from him, not meeting his eye.

He sighed, set down his drink, and drew her against him. As he stood in front of her, he wrapped his hands around the top of her shoulders, gently easing his fingers into the tight muscles.

He could tell she was about to push him away, but then her head dropped back and she gave herself over to his ministrations.

"That feels good," she murmured.

"What have you done to yourself?" he asked. "I've never felt such knots before."

"They're always like this," she said, rolling her head back and forth, providing him better access to the muscles underneath. "Too much... writing for my father."

"What does an architect need such meticulous note-taking for?" Valentine asked with a frown. "You work too hard."

"I enjoy it," she said, but her gaze dropped again to the floor between them and he couldn't shake the sense that she was keeping something from him.

"Lady Fredericka seems lovely," Rebecca said, stepping back away from him and out of his touch.

"Is that what is amiss?" he asked, understanding. If it had been a gentleman he suspected of stealing Rebecca's affections, he could certainly imagine how he would feel. The ball of rage in his gut at the hypothetical thought confirmed it. "Never fear. Lady Fredericka and I have come to the determination that we do not suit."

He could practically see the relief course through her as her shoulders dropped ever so slightly.

"If you are to marry a noblewoman with a significant dowry, I cannot see any others being a better option than she," Rebecca said, her words short and clipped. "She is beautiful, she seems kind, and she is intelligent."

"But she's not you."

Rebecca's head snapped up and she looked at him, the melancholy there apparent.

"I have no dowry, I am not noble, and I must look after my father."

"Your father is a grown man."

"He is," she agreed but said no more.

"I am starting to believe that our separation is ludicrous," he said, voicing the thoughts that had taken hold of him during the previous days and he realized just how much he had missed her.

"Or perhaps what is ludicrous is the fact that we are holding on to hope that there can be a future for us," she said, smiling sadly. "Perhaps there could have been, if you were still a simple pugilist. Or even if you had been born a duke instead of thrust into this life and requiring the guiding hand of a woman who knows it well. But you are trapped between two worlds, and you must embrace who you have become now."

She began to back away slowly toward the door, as though his very presence was what was causing her such pain.

"I must go."

"We are not done with this conversation," he said sternly, to which she did not reply.

"Goodbye, Val," she whispered softly. "Until next time."

And then she was gone, the door shut behind her, empty space where she had been just moments before.

He had just finished downing his drink when another knock sounded on the door, and Val crossed to it expectantly, convinced that Rebecca had returned, having changed her mind following their previous conversation.

But it was his mother.

"Valentine," she greeted him curtly as she walked into the room as though *she* owned this place. "I am pleased with the designs Mr. Lambert has prepared."

"I'm glad to hear it," he said wearily, although to be honest he hardly cared any longer. His mother had taken over anyhow, spending his money as she saw fit, telling the architects what she wanted. "But Mother, we need to make some compromises."

"We wouldn't if you would simply marry as we discussed long ago. I don't understand, Valentine, what is holding you back."

"Just looking for the right woman," he muttered.

"Or, you are looking at the wrong woman," she admonished, pointing a finger at him.

"Excuse me?"

"Oh, I'm not an idiot, Valentine. I know you've had your eye on Miss Lambert."

Well, in truth, he had more than that upon her, but he certainly wasn't going to share that with his mother.

"She is quite striking," his mother continued, waving her hands as she paced around the room. "But I hardly think she has the dowry we require. And while she has spent much of her life around nobility, she has no title herself, and would not further us in any way."

"Tell me, Mother," Valentine said dryly, "am I the one to be married, or are we all going to wed my future bride?"

"Oh, Valentine, do not be daft," she huffed. "You always did manage to bungle every situation. I should think it would be easy. Find a woman with a dowry and marry her. You're a duke, and you are not bad looking. Many women will forgive an unconventional background in order to be called Duchess."

"I would hardly want such a woman who might think that way."

"Valentine, I wish you would just do as your parents bid you," she said with a sigh, collapsing into a chair, the unspoken words between them — that he would do as Matthew always had.

"We are talking about the woman who will join our family and who I will spend the rest of my life with, going to bed with and waking up with every day," he said with frustration. "It is not as though I am simply picking out a bolt of cloth."

"No," she said, standing now and walking over to him, placing her hands on his cheeks. "I know this has been difficult, Valentine, but I must tell you that your father would be so proud of you now."

Her words caused anguish to coil in his gut. It was what he had always wanted to hear, and yet somehow now that she said the words, they didn't provide the fulfillment that he would have assumed.

"Father is not here anymore," he responded without emotion.

"Even so," she said. "It would be what he always wanted of you. We never thought, of course, that the title would find its way to our family, and if it did—"

"Then it would have been Matthew's," he finished for her.

"Yes," she said, her smile sad, and he was reminded of how much she missed his older brother. How much he did, as well. Matthew would have done the right thing. Matthew would have known what to do. Not for the first time, he wished, more than anyone, that Matthew had lived.

"He always loved you so," she continued, and Valentine nodded. As different as they had been, as much as Matthew had always received his parents' approval as opposed to Valentine, who was constantly testing them, he and his brother had gotten along well.

"I am sorry if I seem particularly harsh," she said, resuming her seat, "but I am only doing what is best for our family."

As he should be doing as well, were her unspoken words, as she fixed him with that stare he knew so well.

"I have a suggestion," she said, and Valentine sighed. He was finished with his mother's suggestions.

"What is it?"

"We tell Mr. Lambert that his services are no longer required."

"What?"

"We have a master-builder. We no longer require Mr. Lambert. Pay him, and let him go on his way. Along with his daughter."

"Mother, we have invested so much with him. Do we not want the renovations completed correctly?"

"I am sure that Mr. Burton would be fine on his own."

"Mother," he said, standing and making for the door to signal that this conversation was finished. "You wanted these renovations. If we are going to do them, we are going to do them right."

"But—"

"I must go," he said, refusing to argue with her any longer. "I have a man-of-business to find."

After he ushered her out, he closed the door behind her, wishing he could finish with everything else in his life in such a way.

CHAPTER 21

*R*ebecca now lived for those stolen moments when she would see Valentine at Wyndham House in London. Now that the builders had begun their work, she accompanied her father from time to time to answer any questions and to oversee the construction. Wyndham House was currently the priority before they would continue on to Stonehall.

"That cannot be an enjoyable task," Jemima remarked one day as she and Rebecca stood at the back of the ballroom, staring up at the painter, who was painstakingly covering the ceiling. The workers were currently split between the ballroom and the conservatory. While both Jemima and her mother insisted that Jemima didn't need anything besides an empty room with some tables, Rebecca was adamant that the conservatory work take as much priority as the ballroom. She understood how important it was to have a dedicated workspace. She loved her little study at home, where the sun streamed in upon her desk, angled perfectly from where she could work.

"It is rather tedious work," Rebecca agreed, arching her

already stiff neck to watch the painter, who completed his work on a system of pulleys. "It will be beautiful, however, and completely worth it once it is finished."

"I hope so," Jemima agreed. "Those are not the angels that my mother discussed are they?"

"No," Rebecca said, shaking her head with a smile.

"It almost looks like they have raised their fists at one another."

Rebecca's grin widened ever so slightly.

Jemima turned to her with wide eyes. "You are having him paint pugilists!"

"Perhaps," she said, laughing now, and Jemima took a deep breath, her smile beginning to match Rebecca's.

"My mother is going to absolutely hate it."

"It will be done very tastefully, I can promise you that."

"But Valentine will love it," Jemima finished, and Rebecca's cheeks warmed. She hoped he would. That was her goal. She wasn't sure whether he was going to be upset with her or pleased. She hoped for the latter, but she couldn't be entirely sure.

"I thought you hated the fact that he fights."

Rebecca looked around her for a moment as she considered her answer. The finishing was being added to the pillars, which had already been in place prior to their arrival. The room would be completed before Mrs. St. Vincent's deadline, as they were primarily polishing what had been a large, empty canvas. A few benches around the side, and it would be ready for all of London's finest to attend — including the women who would vie to be the next Duchess of Wyndham.

"I hate the thought that he could be injured. That he is putting himself through it in order to try to fund this dukedom," she finally said. "But if he loves it... well, I understand seeing through on your passions."

Jemima nodded.

"You have done a wonderful job with this house," she remarked, to which Rebecca shook her head, evading the compliment.

"It was already nearly finished anyway," she said.

"Yes, but you have ideas that are quite impressive," Jemima persisted. "I am looking forward to seeing them put into place."

"All in good time," Rebecca murmured. "I do get the sense that your mother no longer welcomes my presence. Why, I'm not entirely sure."

"Well, that's simple," Jemima said, arching an eyebrow. "It is because she knows of the way my brother feels about you."

Rebecca raised her head, meeting Jemima's eye. "I wish I knew."

"Oh, Rebecca," Jemima said, tilting her head as she studied her. "He loves you — I know it, even if he doesn't know it himself."

Rebecca couldn't say a word, her heart lodged in her throat, but she tried her best to swallow it as Valentine entered the room and began walking toward them.

Jemima smiled mischievously.

"Say you will come to the ball."

"Oh, Jemima, I couldn't."

Jemima turned as her brother approached.

"Valentine," she said, swinging her gaze back upon Rebecca. "Tell Rebecca that she must come to the ball."

"Rebecca, you must come to the ball," he repeated dutifully, and Rebecca frowned at him.

"You both know that this ball is not being held for the likes of me."

"You have much more in common with us than any of the other people who will be in attendance," Jemima said. "Even

168

if you do not wish to speak to anyone else, you can sit in the corner with me and Celeste."

"Mother will not be pleased with you ensconced in a corner seat," Valentine teased his sister, and she swatted him.

"I would invite you not to share my plans with her," she dismissed her brother, turning back to Rebecca. "Please, say you will," she said with some desperation. "To have people there I know and trust is the only way I can make it through such a night."

Rebecca stole a glance at Valentine to see what he thought of Jemima's plea, but he wore a similar expression to his sister. Apparently she was not the only one who might welcome Rebecca's presence.

"Very well," Rebecca finally agreed. "As long as your mother doesn't toss me out."

"I'll make sure of it," Jemima said, clapping her hands together and Rebecca took a deep breath. This could be a terrible decision, but in a way, she *was* eager to view the ballroom full of people, to see firsthand what they thought of her design.

She would soon find out if it would be worth it.

* * *

VALENTINE SURVEYED the room in front of him. The ballroom renovation had taken nearly a month to complete — during which time he had taken every opportunity to be at home, just in case Rebecca happened to arrive with her father. His mother thought him ridiculous, and she told him such, but there was nothing he could do about it. He was a man torn by indecision, between following his heart and doing what he thought was the right thing, what his father had always wanted from him, what Matthew would have done.

He and Rebecca had a few stolen moments alone, but it

seemed his mother was always hanging about, or Rebecca's father required her assistance for one thing or another.

Valentine still wasn't completely comfortable with Mr. Lambert. The man he presented himself as did not align with the designs he produced. He was always speaking of past projects, was lost in his affinity for the baroque, and yet the designs were innovative and classical.

Val didn't enjoy not completely trusting someone who worked for him — but he could never fire Mr. Lambert, for that would mean being rid of Rebecca as well, which he could never, ever do, despite his mother's persistence.

Guests had begun to trickle in, and while Val did his utmost to be a most gracious host, he couldn't help his gaze from continuing to wander to the door, awaiting Rebecca.

"Careful, or your neck is going to be stuck like that," Jemima said from the corner of her mouth. She stood beside him near the entryway to the ballroom — which was a masterpiece. Valentine's mother had nearly fainted dead away when she saw the pugilists locked in an everlasting battle in the middle of the ceiling, but when she tried to insist that they be painted over, Valentine had told her that this was one decision that was not hers to make.

It was one thing in this house that spoke to who he was, the new Duke of Wyndham, and he was not going to cover it up. He may have lost most of his identity as Valentine St. Vincent, but these pugilists would not be destroyed.

"Do you think she'll come?" he asked Jemima, not hiding the desperation in his voice as he asked after Rebecca.

"She promised she would, so she will," Jemima said confidently, and he nodded as he greeted another young woman and her mother. This entire ball seemed to be filled with an endless line of eligible young ladies. He expected most of them had significant dowries to accompany their lofty titles, but he couldn't form much more than a passing interest in greeting them. None of them spoke to him.

Until a striking raven-haired vixen approached. She wore a long crimson gown that draped around those hips and the bodice that he knew so well. He wanted to pick her up and spirit her away upstairs to his bedroom. He could only wish that there was a passage from here up to his bedchamber, such as the one from the long gallery to his room at Stonehall. But that was not to be.

"Miss Lambert," he said, a smile gracing his lips. "I am so glad you could join us."

"As am I," added Jemima with a grin.

"Save a dance for me?" Valentine asked, ignoring the knowing smile of his sister next to him.

"I will."

The time between his request and their actual dance seemed interminable. Valentine decided that he didn't particularly enjoy playing host at a ball. Which wasn't a surprise, for he hardly enjoyed attending one as it was.

But at least in the home of others he could leave when he wanted. Here, he was stuck.

He managed to extricate himself from his welcoming duties once the orchestra began to play in earnest, and he quickly sought out Rebecca.

He was well aware that he should be asking for a dance with one of the many young women vying for his attention. In fact, he could actually feel his mother's pointed stare upon him as he crossed the ballroom. But his feet seemed as fickle as his heart, for they led him over to where Rebecca sat against one of the walls with Jemima, her friend Miss Keswick, and Lady Fredericka.

Val knew what his mother was thinking — that he was here for Lady Fredericka. She was a pleasant woman, and one Valentine figured would make a good friend.

But not a wife.

For there was only one woman who so captured his attention.

"Miss Lambert," he said, holding out his hand to her, "may I have this dance?"

She smiled as she rose, placing her hand in his.

"You shall."

He led her out onto the dance floor, aware of the many eyes turned in their direction, but he didn't overly care. If he was to hold this infernal ball, then he would dance with whomever he damn well pleased.

"Are you enjoying yourself?" he asked, forcing himself to make polite conversation when all he wanted to do was crush her into his arms and hold her tight.

"I am enjoying my time with your sister and her friends," she said. "They are not like typical ladies of their station."

"Which is a compliment from you."

"And you as well, I should think."

He chuckled. "You are correct. I have not taken to my new status very well."

"I think you are doing just fine," she said, and Val cringed slightly at her look of admiration. He didn't deserve it. He had done nothing that he should receive any praise for.

They enjoyed an amiable dance, content to be in one another's arms.

"How much talk do you think we would create if we were to dance every waltz together?" he asked, his voice low in Rebecca's ear as they left the dance floor.

She laughed softly.

"Even an unconventional duke such as yourself would have a difficult time in doing such a thing," she said. "You would be the talk of all of London."

"I believe I already am," he said ruefully.

They had nearly made it to the end of the dance floor when a rotund, balding man stopped them.

"I say!" he exclaimed, pointing a finger at Valentine. "I know you."

Val arched an eyebrow. "This is my home," he said carefully, "and as you are an invited guest, I would hope that you know my identity."

The man shook his head. "No, no, I've seen you before. Somewhere else. Somewhere... I've got it!"

Val waited expectantly, his stomach slightly churning. *Don't say it*, he thought. *Please don't—*

"You're the fighter! The pugilist! Val Vincent!"

Heads began to turn their way, and Val could sense Rebecca stiffening beside him.

"You must be mistaken, sir," she said, attempting to defend him. "This is the Duke of Wyndham. He—"

"No, no, there is no doubt about it," the man continued. "I saw Bucky Brown best you two months past, out in Hungerford. Didn't we, Johnson?" he asked one of his companions, who began to nod slowly in recognition.

"You say you are the duke?" the man continued, as a slight crowd began to form around them, more and more eyes turning toward them.

"Your grace!" his mother, her white hair perfectly coiffed and wearing the very finest gown London had to offer, sailed through Valentine's accusers.

"These gentlemen must be mistaken, for I know such a thing could never be. Now, please come with me to greet Lord and Lady Hycliffe and their family. Excuse us!"

Then Valentine was whisked away, with a chorus of onlookers staring after him, Rebecca falling away from his side.

"I am not a child, Mother," he said sternly once they were out of earshot. "I can fight my own battles."

ELLIE ST. CLAIR

"You were doing a terrible job of it," she scolded him. "As it is, your name is going to be on the lips of all in attendance, until this news hits the scandal sheets tomorrow."

"Does it matter?" he challenged her. "They are correct. I am the fighter they are speaking of. It's who I am — more so than the Duke of Wyndham, that is for certain."

She fixed him with a look of disdain.

"You know how upset your father always was about your fighting. Well, I feel no different, as you are well aware. It is because of your fighting that we lost your brother. I told you to be done with it, now that you are the Duke of Wyndham. It will sully your reputation, and the family's along with it, even more so than it already is. Valentine, you *must* find yourself a respectable woman to wed."

"In all honesty, Mother, I care very little about what these people think anymore," he said in exasperation, and she turned to him, aghast.

"But what about me?"

"What about you?" he challenged. "I give you the finest things one could ask for. You are the mother of a duke, and you certainly act in the style one would suppose."

"Well, of course, I do," she said. "Matthew would—"

"I am not Matthew," he said sternly, loud enough that a couple of people turned to look at him, and he quieted his tone so as not to embarrass his mother. "I am sorry, Mother. I wish Matthew was here instead of me, truly I do. But while I may be forced to take his title, I cannot become him. I am who I am — Valentine, the fighter. And it's time I begin to fight for what I want."

She looked at him with equal parts respect and disappointment.

"You are remaining the man we always expected you to be," she said with a sniff. "But there is one thing you cannot argue with."

"And what's that?"

"You need a dowry — and a significant one at that. You best come around and realize that yourself before it's too late."

Then she was off, striding away from him with her nose held high in the air, more lady that she actually was in name.

Aware that he had somehow bungled nearly every situation this evening, Valentine could do nothing but watch her go and wish, not for the first time, that his brother was still with them.

CHAPTER 22

"*M*iss Lambert, might I have a word?"

After stopping for a drink, Rebecca had nearly found her way back to her seat with her newfound friends, but Mrs. St. Vincent intercepted her.

"Of course," she said politely. "Thank you so much for having me this evening."

"Yes, well, my children were insistent," Mrs. St. Vincent said in a way that told Rebecca she clearly would have chosen otherwise. "Miss Lambert," she said, leading Rebecca into a corner of the room, "I am not a fool. I have come to realize that you and my son hold... affection for one another."

Rebecca turned to her, rather stunned. She hadn't realized Mrs. St. Vincent was so perceptive. Or perhaps Rebecca and Valentine had been much more obvious than they would have imagined.

"I suppose there is some truth to that," she said cautiously, unsure of what Valentine would want her to say.

"You must realize, however, that my son is not for you," she continued, quite forthright. "He is a duke now, and while

I am aware that you were raised with much propriety, you are not what he needs, Miss Lambert. You are an intelligent woman and I hope that you can understand this, even if he cannot."

Rebecca's heart and mind swirled with opposing emotions. She was not exactly pleased with Mrs. St. Vincent's words, and yet she was insinuating that Valentine had not given up on her. Of that, Rebecca was more pleased than she could have imagined.

"I believe that is for Valentine to decide," was all she could manage. And truly, she wished he would. He was a grown man, and she was becoming quite frustrated by his lack of ability to stand up to his mother. Though, who was she to tell him such a thing when she had been covering her father's mistakes for years now?

"Men can be idiots," Mrs. St. Vincent said, rolling her eyes. "They cannot be trusted to make the right decisions. Which is why you must do so."

"Oh, Mrs. St.—"

"Don't be a fool, Miss Lambert," she said pointedly. "Besides the fact that you are not of noble birth, you more than anyone should be aware of the costs of living the life we are expected to live. If we want the ability to pay anyone — which would include our architect — then we require funds to do so. Funds that would come from a dowry."

"Or a properly managed dukedom," Rebecca returned.

"That will be some time away," Mrs. St. Vincent said, then narrowed her eyes slightly at Rebecca. "A woman from a family whose father has debts of his own would be the last woman who might make a match with my son."

Rebecca's eyes widened. "How did you know?"

"Do not underestimate a shrewd woman," she said. "Return to your place in the corner, Miss Lambert. It's where you belong."

Rebecca refused to do as she was told by this woman. She, however, was not going to make a scene.

She looked around the room. Mrs. St. Vincent was right about one thing. This was not the place for her — she didn't belong, and never would.

So she left.

* * *

VALENTINE LOOKED EVERYWHERE FOR REBECCA. She was not with his sister, nor was she upon the dance floor. She was not in the drawing room or conversing with anyone else. The last he had seen of her, she was with his mother, which was not a good sign.

As he looked for her in the corridor outside the ballroom and then the parlor, Archie intercepted him.

"Val," he greeted him with a nod. "My apologies, I know I shouldn't be seen around here."

"You are a much more welcome face than anyone else in that ballroom," Valentine said. "Is something amiss?"

"I thought you might be looking for Miss Lambert," he said. "She just left, looking none too pleased."

"She left?"

Archie nodded.

"Damn it," Valentine said, placing his hands upon his hips. "My mother must have said something to her."

"Something that would cause her enough chagrin that she would leave the ball where you are to find your wife?"

"I'm in quite the pickle, Arch," he said with a sigh, and his friend more than his valet grinned at him.

"Don't I know it. You've been in a pickle since the day you were born."

"We're making progress, though, aren't we?" Valentine

asked him, desperate to hear someone speak positively about some aspect of his life.

"You liked the man of business we interviewed, and you have a steward, so we are," Archie nodded slowly. "Though I hate to say it, you will be saddled with some deep debts if you continue spending like you are without receiving a dowry to pay for it all."

Valentine dropped his arms and turned to his friend. "You know where we came from, Archie," he said. "Is it so imperative that I prove myself? Do I need the most impressive homes, the finest garments, the most refined wife? Is my family to be ridiculed without it?"

Archie clasped his hands behind his back.

"You are a long way from respectable," Archie said with a raised eyebrow. "But there is really just one question you need to consider."

"Which is?"

"What is it that really matters to you?"

* * *

REBECCA WEARILY CLIMBED the steps to Wyndham House two days later. Work had been suspended for a few days surrounding the ball, but they needed to check in now with Mr. Burton. Her father had already asked her twice on the carriage ride where they were going, which had Rebecca rather on edge.

And then there was the fact that she couldn't stop thinking about Valentine and his mother's words. The woman knew that she and her father were deeply in debt. Rebecca didn't spend overly long wondering how — it didn't matter, really. The Atticus Project was on public record and the buildings were clearly sitting empty. For now. It might be different if Rebecca's plan had worked, but she — or, that is, her father — had finally received a response from her repeated correspondence to the Crown.

Her plan had not been approved.

It hadn't been rejected either; it was simply not considered anything of importance, apparently, and she was to wait for further review.

Rebecca tilted her head from one side to the other in an effort to crack her neck and break up the many knots that had formed as she had spent more than one restless night hunched over her work. Sleep had eluded her, so she figured she might as well make use of the time awake.

She was paying for it now, however.

She sighed as she and her father entered the house, following Dexter who led them through to the drawing room, though they certainly didn't need a guide. Dexter was pleasant as always, and Rebecca wished she could fall for someone like him — someone who did not have a complex past, present, and future. Someone who didn't have a mother who always wished her son to be what she considered better than he was, but in reality meant that he should be someone he was not.

She knew she had been something of a coward the other night. Rebecca usually preferred to confront her problems directly. But just like a building that was beyond repair, Rebecca had learned when it was time to walk away.

She and her father would finish this project and then be gone.

She hated giving in to Mrs. St. Vincent. But beyond the woman's harsh words, there was truth. Her words were knowledge Rebecca had been aware of from nearly the moment she had met the half-dressed Valentine in his dressing room. She just should have been more careful about giving away her heart.

They heard the pounding coming from the drawing

room, where the builders were currently busy constructing shelving and painting the walls the lovely sea-green Rebecca had chosen.

"This way, Father," she murmured when he began to wander the other way.

He turned to her, confusion on her face. "Where are we, Rebecca?"

Her heart pained her. She hated these moments when he lost himself. She had no idea what caused these momentary memory losses to hit, but she only wished she knew what to do in order to bring him back to her.

All that seemed to work, as far as she could determine, was time.

"We are at Wyndham House," she said quietly, placing a hand on his arm. "We are going to oversee the drawing room. Mr. Burton had some questions."

"Mr. Burton?"

"Yes, the builder. Do you recall meeting with him?"

When her father turned to look at her, his eyes were clouded with confusion, and Rebecca took a breath, reminding herself to have patience. It was no more her father's fault that these episodes hit than her own. She was just facing despair as she had no idea what she was to do. She could hardly continue to try to keep up this charade in public. If Valentine or his mother were to come upon them right now, they would instantly know something was amiss.

"Come, Father, let's go into the drawing room," she said quietly, leading him. She would do the best she could with Mr. Burton and then they would leave as quickly as possible.

Fortunately, her father seemed content, for the moment, to settle himself on a chair and watch the builders and painters at work as Rebecca took a tour about the room.

"It's looking wonderful, Mr. Burton," she complimented him when he came over to greet her.

"Thank you, Miss Lambert," he said. "It's a smart design, taking what the original architect envisioned and incorporating the classical style. Once the furniture arrives, it should come together quite nicely."

"My father is interested to know how the shelving is coming along."

"Quite well," Mr. Burton replied with a nod, "though I do have a question for him."

He looked over at her father and then back at her, and Rebecca had the sense that Mr. Burton had some knowledge of her father's current state of mind, though he didn't voice the thought aloud.

"Perhaps if you put it to me, I can best explain it to him?" she suggested, and he nodded, looking relieved.

"It's the end piece," he explained, showing her two samples of engravings in the wood. "We are unsure if we should finish it with rosettes or diamonds. In addition, we currently have the shelves meeting in the corner, but I thought perhaps they might be better placed on either side of the fireplace."

"An interesting thought, Mr. Burton," she said, picking up the plans from the middle of the room. "My father and I will review them."

She collected her father and the two of them departed for their makeshift workplace in the parlor. While her father admired the view of the windows beyond, Rebecca began to make quick sketches, in an attempt to see the room from different angles and a different light.

Perhaps Mr. Burton had a point, she considered. If the shelves were moved, the window could allow greater light to enter and reflect on—

"Miss Lambert, just what do you think you are doing?"

CHAPTER 23

*R*ebecca froze.

Mrs. St. Vincent was peering over her shoulder, her voice just behind Rebecca's ear. Rebecca had been so engrossed in her sketches that she hadn't heard Valentine's mother approach. She swallowed.

"I am just making a few of the changes my father has suggested," she said quickly, hoping that would appease Mrs. St. Vincent. The woman reached over Rebecca's shoulder and snatched the papers up into her fingers. Rebecca stood quickly, whirling around to face her, but was helpless as Mrs. St. Vincent's eyes roved over them.

"What you just drew…" she began, looking from Rebecca to the paper and back again, "looks to be in the same hand as the rest of the drawings." She looked at the papers spread upon the desks. "As all of the drawings."

"My father and I have a similar hand," Rebecca attempted, looking her in the eye.

"Is this true, Mr. Lambert?" Mrs. St. Vincent asked, her hands on her hips now as she took her focus from Rebecca to her father. Rebecca prayed he wouldn't say anything incriminating.

"Oh, hello," he said with a pleasant smile. "Who might you be?"

"Pardon me?" Mrs. St. Vincent said as Rebecca's heart dropped.

"Lovely to meet you," her father said, holding out his hand. "Are you calling upon Lady Blackburn?"

"Who the devil is Lady Blackburn?" Mrs. St. Vincent asked, turning round eyes onto Rebecca, who was panicking.

"That's enough, Father," she said desperately. "Do stop teasing Mrs. St. Vincent."

"Mrs. St. Vincent!" he said, recognition flaring in his eyes and Rebecca released a sigh of relief.

"I knew a Vincent once. Splendid dog, he was."

The relief fled.

"Miss Lambert." Mrs. St. Vincent turned toward her, her words clipped and her face beginning to turn a mottled red. "Just *what* is the meaning of all of this? Your father seems to be addled in the head!"

"He's not, Mrs. Vincent, he really isn't," Rebecca said, shaking her head, both wishing that Mrs. St. Vincent would forget all of this while at the same time feeling the need to defend her father. So a man forgot something now and again. That didn't mean that he should be sent to Bedlam.

But Mrs. St. Vincent was no longer listening to her. She was turning in circles around the parlor, a hand upon the side of her head.

"Please," she said, closing her eyes and shaking her head, "please tell me that *you* have not been the one designing my homes all this time. That your father, a man renowned over all of England, did not lose his mind as you began to work on the *magnificent* homes of the Duke of Wyndham."

"I have not been the one designing the Duke of Wyndham's homes," she said, emphasizing his name, for, as much as Mrs. St. Vincent seemed to have taken over the design, it was still her son's home. Rebecca only wished he would act like it was. "Not alone, at any rate," she added, unable to completely lie.

"This is unacceptable," Mrs. St. Vincent said as she resumed her frenetic pacing, not even seeing when the door opened and Valentine walked in. "Unacceptable. Why, if we are found out, we will be the laughingstock of all of London. Even more than we already are. New duke, the former pugilist, hires a fraud. Oh, for goodness sake, I—"

"What is happening here?" Val asked, looking back and forth between Rebecca and his mother. Tension began to radiate in the back of Rebecca's shoulder blades, which then wound their way up through her muscles to the sides of her neck.

"What is happening?" Mrs. St. Vincent said, stopping and pointing a finger at Valentine. "What is happening is that I am being proven right. As I always am. You have hired a fraud, Valentine. A fraud! Collect your silly sketchbooks, Miss Lambert, leave this house, and never come back. Do not send an invoice as you will most certainly *not* be paid!"

"Mrs. St. Vincent, I—"

"Will someone tell me what in the *blazes* is going on here?" Rebecca had never heard Val raise his voice in such direct anger before, and she flinched.

"From what I can ascertain, it seems as though Mr. Lambert here has not had the capacity to actually complete any of the designs of your homes himself. Instead, he has been relying on his *daughter*. These drawings aren't from the hand of the architect whose name is renowned over all of London. Oh, no, Valentine, they are from *her*. A woman with hardly any education to speak of, with no experience, and no idea of what the results of her little sketches will be. I can hardly believe it."

Rebecca took slow, deep breaths as Mrs. St. Vincent talked, willing away all of the building resentment. The woman was looking out for the best interests of her children, she reminded herself, though her anger burned hotter than her patience.

"How are we supposed to become respected members of the nobility if we have the worst-designed house in all of London?" Mrs. St. Vincent continued.

Valentine ignored his mother now, his gaze focused intently on Rebecca.

"Is this true?"

She didn't say anything for a moment as she simply stared back at him, wishing that she could run to him and that he would enfold her into her arms and tell her that everything was all right.

But she feared that he would never be telling her that again. Rebecca knew what his reaction was before he said a word. For the look he gave her was filled with such disappointment, anger, and melancholy that his response was evident.

"Is this true?" he repeated, giving each word a sentence all to its own.

"Yes," Rebecca said, louder than she originally intended. Despite the deception, she was proud of what she had done. Her work was good. So good, in fact, that Mr. Burton hadn't even questioned it, nor had Valentine when he had previously reviewed the plans. "Did you like them?"

She knew they did, but she wanted to hear them say it.

"You lied to me," Valentine said instead, ignoring her question. "This entire time… you deceived me. Made me out to be a fool."

"No," Rebecca said firmly, her heart beating quickly now,

her blood pumping through her veins as panic ascended into her throat. "Never, Valentine. That was never my intent. I— I have been working *with* my father for some time now. He is still involved in the designs, he always has been. It's just... well, some days he can do more than others."

She looked back and forth between Valentine and his mother, noting that Jemima had stepped into the doorway, her eyes wide and her expression sympathetic.

"I am no amateur," she said, defending herself, realizing that while she understood Valentine's dismay, she needed him to be supportive of her, to not downplay all the work that she had done simply because she was a woman. She needed the man she loved to support her, her work and her passion, to believe in her and her capabilities. "I have spent my life learning from my father. He is a master architect and he has passed on all of that knowledge to me. How many times did I hear you say how impressive our design was, Valentine? Do you like your lady's maid's new proximity to your chamber, Mrs. St. Vincent? Do you like the openness of the library with the way the doors permit light to enter, the way the mirrors project the greenery around the room? I know you do, Valentine, for you have said so yourself."

She looked intently at one of them and then the other.

"Yes," she said, holding her head high. "Yes, these are primarily my designs. I am proud of them, and you will be proud of your home once they are all implemented."

"You are done here," Mrs. St. Vincent said, lifting her nose and turning from Rebecca to show just how finished she was with her and with the conversation. "You may leave now. Take your things. We will hire a new architect."

"You can't!" Rebecca said, desperation clawing at her throat now at the thought of all of their progress being destroyed. "We are near halfway through completion. This house has already seen the work of two different architects. It would devolve into anarchy if you bring in a third."

"I believe that is for us to determine, Miss Lambert," Mrs. St. Vincent said, and Rebecca turned to Valentine, imploring him to say something, to stand up for her, to agree with her.

But he shook his head.

"I knew something was amiss," he muttered. "Since you arrived at Stonehall, I was aware that something was not as it should be, but I couldn't quite determine what it was. You distracted me. Used me. Ensured that I wouldn't discover what it was you were hiding."

"It was nothing like that," Rebecca said, anger now completely overcoming her fear. "If that is what you think of me, then you know nothing of me at all."

"Apparently, I don't," he said. "My mother is right. You should go."

"Valentine!"

"I will pay you for your work if that is what you are so concerned about," he said dejectedly, and Rebecca balled her hands into fists at her side.

"Don't be despicable," she said. "Keep your money."

"Oh, we have been waiting for our payment, have we not Rebecca?" her father finally chimed in, rising from his place on the sofa. His timing, nor his words, could not have been worse.

"We don't need it, Father," she said tersely.

"Oh, but we do," he said sagely. "You've been saying so for months now. It was why we took on a new project, was it not?"

Rebecca squeezed her eyes shut for a moment, wishing that she could turn back the clocks to but an hour ago when she should have been more careful to not have been discovered. Or that she had told Valentine the entire truth so that it would never have come to this — him suspecting her of ulterior motives.

"Does it really matter that Rebecca was the one doing the work?" Jemima asked softly, entering the room now, and when she came to stand beside her, Rebecca nearly wept with the relief of having someone support her. "The design is what you both were looking for. I, for one, think it to be ingenious."

"This isn't what this is about, Jemima," Valentine said angrily, slashing his hand through the air. "It's about her deception."

"Perhaps she was worried this is what would have happened, had you found out about it — that they would be turned away."

"And lose the paycheck they so desperately need," Valentine retorted, and Rebecca placed her hand on Jemima's arm.

"Thank you, Jemima, but it's all right. I understand."

"It's not all right," her new friend said, and a small bit of Rebecca's heart began to mend itself back together — until she realized that she would likely never be seeing Jemima again, not with the rift that had just been torn between Rebecca and the St. Vincents.

"It is," Rebecca said, attempting to lift the corners of her mouth. "We should be going now. Come, Father."

"Where are we going?" he asked, but Rebecca responded simply by taking his arm and leading him to the door.

"I shall walk you out," Mrs. St. Vincent said, and Rebecca's heart hardened.

"That is really not necessary," she said tersely, though still politely.

"I insist," she said, placing a hand on Rebecca's back and nearly pushing her out the door when Rebecca attempted to turn to look back at Valentine. All was silent for a moment as they walked down the hallway.

"I know what you were here for, Miss Lambert," she said. "The title of duchess is a high-minded one for any woman, but especially for a common one. I should know. Valentine, however, is already spoken for. You can look for his betrothal in the newspaper any day now."

She stopped at the doorway, the slightest bit of regret touching her face.

"I apologize that it has come to this, Miss Lambert. But a mother must always put her children first, no matter what. Farewell, now. My best to you, Mr. Lambert. I hope you are well soon."

And with that, Rebecca found herself deposited on the top of the lofty stairwell, her father at her side, her heart wrenched open, and her emotions frayed.

As she called a hack, she replayed the entire scene within the house, torn between guilt at Valentine's words — she *had* deceived him, though not intentionally — and ire that he hadn't stood up for her, hadn't understood.

She stole a glance at her father, who was looking about him, admiring the view on either side of them in this most prestigious of London neighborhoods, and she swallowed back the tears that threatened, determined not to let them fall until she was alone. Her only current blessing was that her father was unaware of the depths of her misery.

All he had worked for was falling down around him, and he had no idea. For one word on his current state of mind and he would be finished. His legacy, his reputation would be destroyed. Rebecca would never work again.

And they would be sunk.

Rebecca had no idea just what she was supposed to do now.

CHAPTER 24

*T*he ledger of accounts sat on one side of the table. Her sketch pad sat on the other.

Rebecca knew which one she *should* be dealing with, for the other no longer mattered. And yet she couldn't help but open up the pad to a blank sheet of paper. She released her mind from all of her tribulations and allowed the pencil to wander over the page. Left to freely roam, it began to draw the place where Rebecca always returned when she needed comfort — a little garden that had planted in her mind. She wasn't sure where it had come from as she had never seen one quite like it. There was a stream that meandered over rocks, cascading down a hill that was filled with wildflowers. A stone arch crossed the water, leading to a tiny pond at the bottom.

Blooms of all colors laced the arch, then poured down into a beautiful flower garden below. She would build a little gazebo beyond, one in which she could set up an easel and work while the beauty of the outdoors surrounded her.

She sighed as she sat back and pictured it. If only such a reality could possibly exist for her. As she looked around her,

ELLIE ST. CLAIR

however, she knew that the greater outcome for her life was one in which she would be removed from even this home. It wasn't much — rooms she and her father had inhabited when not living elsewhere on a job — but it was much better than where they may be relegated to if they were forced to try to pay the debts that they owed from the Atticus Project.

Rebecca laid her head in her hands. Oh, why had Father been so insistent? Perhaps it was the beginnings of when he began to lose control of his mind. He allowed his aspirations to outweigh any judgment he had ever possessed. She massaged her thumbs into the back of her neck, and then jumped when she heard their lone maid call to her with a "Miss Lambert?"

"Oh! Yes, Hilda?"

"There are women here who have come to call. I put them in the drawing room."

"Thank you, Hilda."

Rebecca sighed, looking down at herself to assess whether she was fit for company. She supposed there wasn't much she could do, at any rate, for they were already here and knew she was within.

She re-pinned her hair before leaving the solace of the study and entering the drawing room, taking a breath when she saw Jemima, Freddie, and Celeste.

"Good afternoon, ladies," she said, fixing a smile on her face. "How lovely to see you."

Jemima rose and took Rebecca by the hands.

"I am so sorry that my mother and my brother were awful to you. You didn't deserve that. Come, sit."

Rebecca dutifully sat.

"I hope you don't mind, but I told Freddie and Celeste what happened. They are quite sympathetic to your plight."

Jemima scrunched her nose in worry at sharing the secret, but Rebecca no longer cared. Mrs. St. Vincent was likely to tell all of their duplicity anyway, so what did it matter that these women knew the truth?

"It's fine," Rebecca said, with a sad smile for the other women who, as Jemima said, looked to be pitying her. "Thank you for your understanding. Though, Jemima, they had a point. I deceived them. They didn't hire me. They hired my father."

"How is he?" Jemima asked, furrowing her brow.

"He is fine today," Rebecca said carefully. "Just this morning he was actually on a tirade about the loss of our commission, which is his usual self."

"I am sorry about that as well," Jemima said. "Mother has already begun suggesting other architects to Val, but he has ordered Mr. Burton to continue on with your plans, you will be happy to know — at least for Wyndham House in London."

"I *am* happy to hear it, actually," Rebecca said with surprise. "It will be a beautiful home."

"It is a shame, really," Celeste chimed in, "that your plans would be disregarded just because you are a woman. For isn't it women who spend the most time running the household, who best understand what is required, and what other women would see as beautiful?"

"One would imagine," Freddie said wryly, "but most do not think that way."

"The thing is, Rebecca," Jemima said slowly, taking her lip between her teeth for a moment, "my brother has the worst fear of disappointing people."

"I gathered that."

"Has he ever told you why?"

Rebecca thought back to the many nights spent together, lying in his bed at Stonehall. "Yes," she said. "I know that you had a brother, Matthew, who was supposed to follow in the family tradition but that he died when he was mistaken for

Valentine. Your mother has never quite gotten over it, and Val has never ceased blaming himself."

"Yes," Jemima said, looking down, and Rebecca felt like a boor for bringing up her brothers and all that had happened. Of course, Jemima would miss her brother just as much. "Matthew was the best of us. He always did what was expected of him, was intelligent, pleasant, and Father's image in every way. Valentine is nothing like him and never has been, and my parents — especially my Father — made sure that he knew it. When Matthew died, they were distraught, although of course none more than Valentine. He has never forgiven himself and has spent his life since trying to make up for Matthew's loss. Mother ensures that Valentine never forgets how much Father despaired of Valentine and his chosen profession and that Matthew would still be alive if it wasn't for Valentine's fights. Val now has a hard time forgetting that he need not *be* Matthew."

Rebecca nodded slowly, understanding.

"Luckily," Freddie said pluckily, "Our mothers have decided that *I* am the one he should marry. And I am never one to accept what others tell me is the truth. Valentine and I simply do not suit. He is an amiable gentleman to be sure, and I think that the two of you, Rebecca, would be quite happy together should he ever overcome his past."

"If he does not marry you," Rebecca said, tamping down the jealousy that threatened at even the thought of Valentine marrying another, "then his mother will simply find another young woman who is much more dutiful. Not that you aren't — I certainly didn't mean to suggest that."

"It's fine," Freddie said waving a hand in the air. "Dutiful would not be a word to describe me, although my mother is lovely and I do my best to keep her happy. Marrying a man I do not love, however, will simply not do."

"So the question is, Rebecca," Celeste said, leaning

forward with elbows on her knees, her wide green eyes seemingly looking through into Rebecca's soul, "what can we do to help you?"

Rebecca looked at each of them in turn, the three of them all staring at her with such compassion, such concern. She did what she had been holding back from for weeks now. She began to cry.

"Oh, Rebecca!" Jemima said, looping an arm around her. "I am so sorry. We never meant to upset you."

"It is not that," Rebecca said, wiping at her eyes as she sniffed. "I just... I have never had anyone care for me in such a way before. Who are concerned that my own interests are met, who worry about how I feel and how to help things improve. But the truth of it is... I just don't think anything can be done. If there could be, I would have attempted it myself already. But Valentine needs to come to his own conclusions. He knows how I feel about him."

"But does he?" Jemima asked, tilting her head to the side as she considered Rebecca. "I wonder. He is being stubborn, and he is under the impression that you might have used him. If he knew how you truly felt..." she shrugged, "it might change things."

Rebecca pressed her lips together, nodding slowly. "Perhaps. But despite that, he must marry someone with a dowry. I have only debt."

"From the Atticus Project," Jemima said, nodding, then quickly described the situation to the other women.

"You have not advanced your concerns?" Jemima asked.

"No," Rebecca said, shaking her head. "No one seems to care, and we need Crown approval to hold a lottery."

"It is a fine idea," Freddie remarked.

"Thank you," Rebecca said. "But it will remain just that — an idea — unless we can move forward, and I have simply encountered one brick wall after another."

ELLIE ST. CLAIR

"Leave that with me," Jemima said firmly, nodding at Rebecca's skeptical gaze. "I cannot promise anything, but at least let me try."

"Very well," Rebecca said with a shrug. It wasn't as though she had any other option. "Jemima, I hate to ask you this, but has your mother—"

"Shared anything about you? No," Jemima frowned. "At least, not that I know of. My mother thinks she is doing what is best for us, what is best for Val, but sometimes she doesn't quite understand how to go about it. She isn't from the aristocracy, and now to be suddenly thrust into this life, she is trying to navigate it by doing what she feels is best, despite the fact that her thoughts might actually be to the contrary."

"Don't give up, Rebecca," Celeste said with a soft smile. "Stars often shine brightest on the darkest night."

"That's very romantic," Rebecca said with a small laugh.

"It's the truth," Celeste insisted. "I've seen it often enough myself."

Rebecca reflected on those words as she said farewell to her new friends a short time later. Friends. She couldn't remember the last time she could have attributed the word to any woman and truly meant it. It warmed her heart, and in all honesty, she did feel a great deal better than she had before they arrived.

If only they had actually been able to help change her situation. But the truth was, all remained the same.

Most hope was lost.

There was only one thing she could do, and that was take Jemima's advice — and show Valentine just how she really felt about him.

CHAPTER 25

"You know, I could find you a fight that would actually bring you in some decent prize money," Archie said as he helped Valentine into his jacket.

"Not today," Valentine said, buttoning it himself. "I feel like punching a lord or two instead."

"Well, that *will* be oddly satisfying to watch," Archie laughed as he found Val's cravat. "I must say, you have well played the part of the brooding duke."

"I am not brooding," Valentine defended himself, to which Archie raised an eyebrow.

"Call it what you want," Archie said, "but you are pining for Miss Lambert."

"I am not," Val countered. "I am angry."

"Because a woman designed your house?"

Valentine brusquely shook his head. "You would think that of me after all my sister does? Hardly. I am well aware that a woman's intelligence can not only rival but best a man's. No, Archie. It was the deception. She used me. Her own father admitted that they needed the money. She was

ELLIE ST. CLAIR

worried that if I knew the truth, I would be rid of her, and so she distracted me, played me for the fool I am."

Archie was silent for a moment as he chose a pair of cufflinks.

"Are you sure that was her aim?" he asked, turning around, earning himself a glare.

"Of course," Valentine bit out. "This is why I choose to surround myself with only those I trust. I have learned my lesson now — the hard way. People take advantage of those in positions of power. Especially those like me, who are not cunning enough to see through others."

Archie crossed his arms and leaned back against the wall.

"You're a bit too distrustful."

"You should be grateful — it's why you have this job."

Archie snorted. "Do you think I am here because I need your money?"

"Is that not why everyone is here?"

Archie came and stood beside him, looking into the mirror with him.

"I am here, Valentine, because you needed a friend."

At that, Archie stepped away, clearing his throat. It was the most he and Valentine had ever expressed emotion to one another, and he was obviously done with the conversation.

"You also needed your second, although I can hardly play that role at Jackson's. Best be going now, or else you will miss your match."

Valentine gave a curt nod and was out the door, ready to be rid of his emotions the only way he knew how.

* * *

"You cannot be seriously considering following through with the house plans."

198

Valentine wearily rubbed a hand over his face as he looked up at his mother, who had insisted that he take dinner with her. Jemima, unfortunately, was nowhere to be found. He had already checked the conservatory which, he had to admit, was a stroke of genius with its conversion into a laboratory among the newly planted greenery. Her tables were empty of experiments, however, her liquids, instruments and everything else that he had no actual idea of what they were used for, were awaiting her return.

Finally, he'd found Dexter, who had told him that his sister had gone out.

So here he was, alone with his mother.

"We have a fine set of plans," he said as patiently as he could while he speared peas onto his fork, forcing his bruised knuckles to grip the utensils tightly. "I see no reason to commission another to alter them once more."

"But Valentine," she persisted, banging the end of her fork against the table, "these were designed by a woman and a madman! Why, if word got out—"

"How would word get out, Mother?"

She hesitated. "These things always do."

"Not if you do not say anything."

"But—"

Valentine sighed as he looked around the dining room. The builders had yet to touch this room, but he could already see Rebecca's ideas upon the walls, even if they had not been incorporated. She was everywhere throughout this house, and it was driving him mad. If he entered the drawing room, he saw her in the sea-green walls, the bold contrast of the vivid colors and the scenes from classical antiquity she had envisioned upon the ceiling. If he walked through the ballroom, there she was, right up to the depiction of him painted upon the ceiling as a pugilist. He couldn't even go into the parlor, for he could see her bent over the desk, hard at work.

"Promise me, Mother, that you will not share anything about the Lamberts."

She lifted her nose in the air, which annoyed Valentine. She was a physician's wife as much as she was the mother of a duke, but she seemed to have forgotten that.

"Valentine, you wanted her gone as much as I did if I remember correctly."

Val pushed his plate away, no longer hungry.

"I'm tired, Mother, and I am finished with this conversation and with this dinner."

"You really shouldn't go to that boxing club of yours," she said. "I thought you were done with that life, now that you are a duke."

"It's not the *life* that I needed to leave, Mother," he said. "What you will never understand is that I love the sport, that I need to be moving, or else I feel like I will wither away to nothing. I am fortunate that I can still be part of it, even in my new position of duke, don't you understand that? And never fear, it is perfectly respectable to take part at Jackson's, no matter who I am."

She sniffed.

"Very well. As long as you keep up appearances."

"You know what, Mother?" he said, his patience having reached its limit. "I could care less about appearances."

"Valentine!"

"Did you care so much when you were a physician's wife? You were respectable then. I was the only blight upon the family name. Now I am the one who *holds* the family name, and I can bloody well do what I please with it."

"My word! I—"

He stood now, pushing his chair back and throwing down his serviette. "If you say a word to anyone about Rebecca and her father, then I will see to it that all of these things you have become so enamored with will no longer be available to you. Your extravagant gowns, your new carriage, the jewels you have purchased to wear around your throat — I will sell all of it to pay these debts."

"Sit down, Valentine, this instant. You are acting like—"

"Like what? A boor? A commoner? Well, that is what I am."

"You are the Duke of Wyndham," she said, standing, her fury barely contained. "It is time you act like it. You have been such a—"

"A disappointment? Well, guess what? I'm used to it. And I do not care any longer. Be disappointed in me all you like, Mother. For you know what? I am disappointed in myself as well. Disappointed that I have tried to live up to a man who would never have approved of me. That I continue to try to do what he would have wanted of me, despite the fact that he is no longer even here. That I have allowed my mother to make me feel as though I am not worthy when all I have ever done is to try to provide for myself and this family by doing what makes me happy. That I have cared enough about what others may think to send this family into further debt. It ends today. No more new things until our debts are paid. No renovations to Stonehall. Wyndham House will be finished, but as frugally as possible. I will never fix what happened to Matthew and will regret it for the rest of my life, but I cannot become him."

He began to stride from the room, unable to look back at his mother's stricken face.

"And no marriage to Lady Fredericka Ashworth!"

* * *

"THAT WAS QUITE THE SPECTACLE," offered a feminine voice from the doorway of his study.

"Thank you for providing me your support," Valentine responded sarcastically.

He sent his foot back to the floor, sending the front two legs of his caned klismos desk chair down against the hardwood with a crash as he regarded his sister over fingers steepled in front of him.

"I didn't feel the need to interfere," Jemima said with a slight smile as she entered the room and took a seat in the cushioned open armchair in front of his desk. "You were doing just fine on your own. Good for you, Valentine, for finally standing up to Mother. It was about time."

"Easy for you to say."

She shrugged. "Mother ignores me. Which I am more than happy with. But she has asked too much of you. So did Father. You need to stop holding yourself responsible for Matthew's death. He would never have wanted you to suffer so, to try to be someone you are not. You are not Matthew, and you never will be." She leveled him with her gaze. "But you are an idiot."

"I am already aware of that, Jemima. I do not need your reminder, but thank you anyway."

"That is not what I mean, and you well know it," his sister answered. "When it comes to Rebecca, you are being a stubborn bull. She never meant to deceive you. You should know better than that."

He hated being chastised like a child.

"She doesn't care for me, Jemima. She never did. She was simply using me, and it hardly matters."

"You are wrong," she said softly, tilting her head toward him. "She cares for you very much."

"She is telling you what you want to hear," he countered. "She is deceptive."

"She was only trying to protect her father," Jemima said, leaning forward now, her posture no longer laid back.

"Wouldn't you do the same? As it is, you have been trying to please our parents for years now, and Father is not even alive. She was trying to keep her own father's legacy intact while using the talent she has been given. It hasn't been easy for her."

"She still shouldn't have used me to try to advance herself."

"Rebecca was just trying to survive, Valentine. Just as you are."

He sat back in his chair once more as Jemima's words began to resonate. Was she right? *Could* she be right? Did Rebecca actually feel something for him, or was he a place-holder, as he seemed to be for everyone else?

"It is unfortunate that her creativity is wasted," he said, looking at the plans set before him on his desk. She had done it all rather brilliantly, but he knew that no one would ever agree to a young woman, trained only by experience, designing for them.

"It doesn't have to be," Jemima said. "You could allow her to finish her work here. And there is something else she could use your help with — something that would free some of the burdens she has been carrying."

Valentine eyed her suspiciously. He had a feeling this had been Jemima's angle since she had walked into the room.

"Go on."

"Did she tell you about the houses her father built upon speculation — an entire neighborhood full of them?"

"The Atticus Project? She did. I went to see them for myself. They are ingenious, though not overly practical, and built too far from the West End for most to be interested in them. They are also unfinished."

"They haven't sold, and Mr. Lambert ran out of money to complete them."

"So I am told. I thought Mr. Lambert — though I suppose

it was all Rebecca — had an idea to sell tickets for them as some kind of lottery."

"That is Rebecca's plan, yes, but she requires Crown approval and thus far, her request has been deemed unimportant. She may never receive an answer."

"You want me to intercede on her behalf, don't you?" He shook his head. He should have learned by now to never underestimate his sister.

"You are a duke, Valentine. You are as close to the Crown as anyone can get. Can you at least write some sort of correspondence?"

He tapped his pen on the desk.

"That, I suppose I can do."

He was still unsure about Rebecca's motivations and her thoughts regarding him, but he was certain of a few other things.

First, she deserved to have her work seen. Secondly, her father was — or had been — a brilliant architect at one point in time and that legacy should remain unscathed.

And third?

He loved her, whether he liked it or not.

CHAPTER 26

"*P*ost for Mr. Lambert. Oh, and a letter for you as well, Miss Lambert."

Rebecca stood and took the correspondence from the butler, who was aware that while her father's name was on the house and most of the post, she was the one who looked after everything now.

Her heart quickened when she saw the seal on the back of the envelope, and she sat down at her desk with trembling fingers.

Mr. Lambert,

I am pleased to inform you that your request to sell tickets to a lottery for the homes of the Atticus Project has been approved.

There was a great deal of fine print below regarding when and where the lottery was expected to take place, but Rebecca disregarded it for a moment as she stood and lifted her hands in the air in victory as she spun in a circle. Finally,

finally, something had gone right. She sat down once more, pressing the paper against her chest as she squeezed her eyes shut.

Thank you, God.

It took a while for her to remember the second envelope, and she opened it quickly, seeing it was from Wyndham House. Was it Valentine's mother demanding the payment he had sent be returned?

No, it was in Jemima's script.

REBECCA,

Valentine would never admit this, but it was he who went to the Crown to see to your request. He is a stubborn man, but I know he deeply cares for you. I hope to see you soon,

Jemima

VALENTINE HAD SPOKEN to the Crown for her? Duke or not, one could ask only so many favors, and he had used one of them on her. She took a breath. What did that mean? Did he care for her, as Jemima said? Was he willing to forgive her deception?

She had to be sure that after all he had done, this crazy scheme of hers worked. She had a plan in place, which she was eager to begin, but first, she had something else to finish. Something much more important.

Rebecca had no idea if, following Jemima's visit, Valentine had ever hired another architect. Valentine had sent payment for the work they had done, but every time she looked at the banknote sitting on her desk, her stomach became empty and hollow with guilt.

If he had decided to follow their plans, though, there was one room that was not yet completed. Until now.

It had required quite a few meetings with Archie following her disgraceful exit. There was a third room on the other side of the manor, across from the ballroom and closer to the drawing room. In the original drawings, it seemed to be a gallery of sorts, but Rebecca had another use for it.

She sat back and looked upon it with a smile. One more meeting and it would be complete.

She only hoped Valentine would realize what it was — a declaration of her love.

* * *

"VALENTINE, I am *so* glad you are home."

"Yes, Mother?"

He was spending more and more time at Jackson's, the only place he seemed to fit in between the world he came from and where he had found himself. Soon he would have to assume his seat in the House of Lords, but he was waiting as long as he could before doing so. It did not seem an overly enjoyable way to spend one's time.

"Mr. Burton is doing something in the gallery room and I am not allowed entrance. In my own home, Valentine! You *must* go speak to him."

Valentine frowned. "I am sure he has a good reason, Mother."

It wasn't that he overly cared about the sculpture gallery. It was more so that he didn't have many additional funds set aside to fund another room's renovation. As it was, the existing work on Wyndham House was all he could pay for before diving deeper into debt.

Valentine went looking for his master builder in the east wing of the manor.

"Mr. Burton?"

He was met with silence until he finally pushed open the door.

The room seemed bigger than it had before, but perhaps it was due to what filled it. Ropes were strung from stakes that had been built into the floor, sectioning off the perfect-sized boxing ring. Next to it were bags suspended from the ceiling, with a curtain at the back of the room likely for dressing. Chairs lined one wall, underneath paintings of pugilists as well as landscapes that looked suspiciously like Hungerford.

There was a plaque adorning one wall, right in the center, which Val neared in order to read the inscription.

Home of Valentine St. Vincent
Champion Pugilist
Duke of Wyndham

"What in the...?"

He heard a creak in the floorboards behind him and turned around, expecting to see Mr. Burton.

"Rebecca."

She stood in the doorway, a beautiful angel in a muslin cream dress. Her long dark hair was pulled back away from her face, leaving her hazel eyes shining upon him. Her red lips drew him in, but she was worrying them with her teeth, likely concerned about what his reaction might be upon seeing her here.

She needn't have worried.

"This... this room," he said turning around and holding out his hand toward it. "You did this?"

She took a tentative step toward him.

"I did," she said, nodding her head. "You needn't worry about the expense. It is a gift — I will look after it. Father and I have been fortunate, as our lottery plan is going forward.

We received Crown approval for the project." She tilted her head. "How do you think that came to be?"

He shrugged nonchalantly. "I wouldn't know."

"Are you sure?" she asked, raising her eyebrows. "This from the man who would like trust and honesty?"

He grinned sheepishly, unable to hold back his joy upon seeing her, despite all of the upheaval that existed between them.

"Very well," he said. "I may have had something to do with it. But it was nothing, honestly."

"You're wrong," she said softly, taking another step, one that he found himself matching. "It is much more than nothing. It is everything to my father, and therefore everything to me."

"He deserves for his legacy to remain," Valentine said gruffly. "And you deserve for your work to be seen — just as you deserve to be happy."

"I want the same for you," she said with a sad smile.

"There is a problem with that," he said, taking her hands in his as he finally reached her. "I cannot be happy without one thing."

"What's that?"

"You."

Her eyes flew up to meet his, tears swimming within their depths.

"I miss you so much, Valentine, truly I do, but I cannot be with you any more without the promise for something more between us. I so appreciate all that you have done for me, and I did this because I wanted you to know just how much I lo— care for you."

His heart began to warm within his chest before the heat radiated out through his limbs.

"What was that you were going to say?"

"That I care for you."

He raised an eyebrow, silently urging her to tell the truth.

"Fine," she grumbled, looking down, refusing to meet his eyes. "I love you. I love you, Valentine St. Vincent, but it doesn't matter. It can't. I'm not the woman that you need."

He brought her hands to his lips, kissing each knuckle in turn.

"You're the one that I want, though. I love you, too, Rebecca."

Her smile was tremulous as she looked at him, her eyes watery once more.

"Marry me, Rebecca."

"What?" her lips parted as she gasped.

"Marry me. If I have to be a duke, then I choose you to be my duchess."

"I am not titled. I will not help you gain any recognition. I do not have a dowry, though I, at least, no longer have any debt."

"I'll give you a title. I'll pay off my debt. And the only recognition I want is from you."

She swatted him, shaking her head. "Don't tease me, Valentine. You have been telling me that is what you need since I met you. Nothing else is so important to you as that."

"It was important to my mother, and apparently would have been to my father. Ever since Matthew died, all I have done is tried to be the man that he would have been. It's you — and some reminders from others who know me well — who has finally made me realize that I cannot return to the past and change what happened to Matthew, and punishing myself for his loss will accomplish nothing. I can still be myself and make them proud. And being myself means being with you."

"Truly?" she asked, her hands gripping his, and he nodded. "Absolutely."

"What about... the fact that I was less than honest with

you? I am sorry, Valentine, truly I am. I never knew I would fall in love with you, and I didn't mean to deceive you in such a way. My intention was to help my father, but his mind was failing more and more quickly, and the next thing I knew I was doing all of the design, but I didn't want to tell you as I was afraid that you would think less of me. Once I knew that you wouldn't, I was worried you would be angry with me for lying to you, which you were, so I—"

He placed a finger on her lips to stop her flow of words.

"I know," he said, letting his hand fall back down to grasp hers once more. "I was angry, I will admit that. I have become rather paranoid in this new life of mine. Too many people have been proven to be taking advantage of me. It's why I only hire those who knew me before I became duke. You were the first person I took a chance on, and when I thought you had deceived me, well... my anger got the best of me. It usually does."

"I am *truly* sorry," she said, her expression so remorseful that he could do nothing but release a low chuckle.

"I know, Rebecca," he said, lifting her chin with his finger. He didn't want her to feel such shame again. He had suffered from it enough throughout his life that he didn't wish it upon the woman he loved. "And I understand."

"You do?"

"I do," he nodded.

"But what about your own debts? The dowry that you sorely need? I may be able to come up with enough, depending on how well this lottery goes, but I'm not sure it will ever equal that of a titled lady's."

He shrugged. "Well, first, we just may have to wait on some of those wonderful suggestions for Stonehall. I am not saying that we never do them but we—"

"Be prudent and wait," she said, nodding with a smile. "I agree. And while Wyndham House does need to be finished, I have already planned it as inexpensively as possible, if you look—"

"I know, Rebecca," he said with a small smile. "I noticed. And I appreciate it. I appreciate you, and the care you took for what I needed. But besides that, I believe I have found a man of business who will care much more than the old duke's ever did. And stewards that are honest, who will manage the tenants with a firm yet understanding hand."

"I'm glad," Rebecca said with a true smile now. "You are a good judge of character, Valentine, and while I know this might not have been the life you imagined, you will do a fine job of it."

"I'll keep fighting for it, anyway — that, you can be sure of," he promised. "I will also fight for you."

"What are you talking about?" she said, her brow furrowed in confusion. "You already have me."

"I mean that I will fight for you to be able to continue to do what you love," he said and her eyes widened. "In all honesty, as a woman without formal training, you will likely never receive the commissions your father did. But I will make sure all know that you are the genius behind our own designs and I will solidly support you in whatever way I can."

Rebecca cupped his cheek.

"Thank you," she said, her smile turning from sad to one that showed her perfect, even teeth. "I do appreciate it."

"Care to show me how much?

CHAPTER 27

$\mathcal{R}$ ebecca had seen that wide, wicked grin on Valentine's face before.

She knew exactly what it meant.

And she loved it.

"I would be happy to show you," she said, matching his grin with one of her own. "Though I should hardly think that a boxing ring would be the place to do so, although I can see how that might fulfill some sort of wild fantasy of yours."

He leaned back and laughed.

"You have no idea," he said, trailing a finger down her cheek, "but, as it happens, there is a stairwell in this wing of the house that we could use without notice." He cocked his head to the side. "Besides the odd servant who might be about, so we will just have to be careful, my future duchess."

"That seems so strange to hear."

"Now you know how I have felt for so long."

He slid his hands down her arms to her elbows until he captured her waist with them, drawing her closer toward him until they were standing flush against one another.

"I cannot tell you how much I've missed you," he said,

resting his forehead against hers. "I saw you everywhere I looked in this house."

"That's what you get for falling in love with the architect," she smiled against his lips. She could feel his answering smile just moments before his lips came down upon hers, seizing her with more possessiveness than he ever had before. Rebecca understood it, for the same sense coursed through her. Every time they had been together before, there was a finality to it, as though it might be the last time they would ever be together.

But now — now, everything had changed.

She slid one hand around the back of his head, holding him close as they explored, tasted, and promised one another of all that was to come. Valentine bent and tucked one arm underneath her knees, picking her up without breaking contact. Finally, he ended the kiss, though Rebecca was aware it was only for a moment as he strode over and opened the door of the boxing room. He looked quickly back and forth in front of them, and, seeing no one about, had her up the stairs and down the corridor to his chamber so fast she hardly had time to be concerned about who might see them.

All worry fled, however, when he closed the door behind them, leaving the two of them alone in his room.

"It's been a while since I've been in here," she said, inching back toward the bed.

"We've come a long way since the first time we met," he acknowledged, and she nodded slowly as her fingers came to the buttons of his shirt, for he wore no jacket and waistcoat. She liked that he refused to succumb to all that was expected of him and his station.

"When I saw you without your shirt on, I couldn't take my eyes off of you," she said, unable to meet his gaze as her cheeks warmed.

"Oh, and now you can?" he asked, laughter in his voice.

"It's not that," she said, baring his chest. "It's only that now I know you so much better. When I close my eyes I can see your skin, know where your scars are located, and where the muscles meet one another. My fingers remember the planes of your chest, the ridges of your abdomen."

"I must say, I do enjoy your hands upon me more than any other," he said as he began to pull the pins out of her hair, and she stiffened at the thought of him with another woman. "Although most of the hands on my body these days are the knuckles of those who are attempting to beat me senseless."

Rebecca wasn't sure if his explanation was much better than imagining that of another woman, but it made much more sense now.

"Then there is you," he said, turning her around, his fingers coming to the buttons that crept up the back of her dress as his lips dusted her neck. "I do not think there is another woman's body in all of the world that is as perfect as yours."

"Oh, stop," she said, beginning to step away but he held her back firmly in place.

"It is the truth," he said, his breath on her neck and shoulder causing her to shiver, which he misinterpreted.

"Are you cold?"

"Not at all," she said, leaning back against him so that they were skin-to-skin. "In fact, I cannot remember the last time I've been so warm."

His hands skimmed up her back and over her shoulders to her neck.

"As tense as ever," he murmured, digging his thumbs into her tight muscles, the relief and pleasure at the pressure nearly bringing her to her knees as she groaned.

"Your turn," she said, turning around, but he shook his head.

"That was not exactly what I had in mind for myself," he said, to which she raised an eyebrow.

"No?"

"No."

He took steps toward her, forcing her to back up until her legs hit the edge of the bed.

Rebecca looked above her.

"The detailing of the headboard and the posts of this bed is exquisite," she remarked, running her fingers over the etching. "When do you suppose it was—"

"Rebecca."

"Yes?"

"Perhaps we can discuss the history of my bed at a later time. At the moment there are far more urgent requirements for the bed that do *not* include the engravings."

"Ah— yes. That's right. Silly me."

"Do you think," he leaned down over top of her, "I could attempt to distract you, for just a moment, from your endless study?"

"You may try,'" she said a smile coming to her lips. "Though I'm not sure what else could be as titillating as rosewood carvings."

"So you have continued to study them, haven't you?" Valentine asked, looking heavenward. "Lord, help me. My bride finds my bed more interesting than the man who would attempt to join her in it."

Rebecca laughed as she reached out and pulled him down toward her.

"You are the most aggravating man."

"Better get used to it," he said with a laugh, "for you are stuck with me now."

She kissed him firmly in response.

They tumbled down onto the bed together. When Valentine gathered her into his arms, Rebecca had never before felt so complete. She could allow herself to rely on someone else, to share her worries and her fears, to take on her burdens and lift up her dreams.

She trailed her fingers over his defined shoulder, his powerful biceps muscle, taking in all of him that was both fascinatingly beautiful and also spoke to who he was and what he loved to do. She might never understand it, but she loved him for pursuing what was true to him.

He caught her fingers, kissing each one of them in turn before taking one in his mouth and then slowly releasing it. Rebecca's breath caught, and suddenly all of the humor between them fled.

"I think I can convince you that I'm worth it," he said, his voice husky.

"I have known your worth since the moment I met you," she said, taking his face in her hands and looking at him intently. "Don't you forget it."

Their mouths fused together as they held onto one another with the passion that had quickly overtaken them. Their joining was not slow or careful, but it was full of all the love flowing between them.

Valentine's hands, the large and rough hands of a fighter, turned soft and gentle as they roved over Rebecca's body before finding their place at her center near where they joined together, where he caressed her until she was nearly screaming with urgency to find her release.

"Valentine," she groaned as he pumped into her, moments before her world exploded into pieces around her. Valentine soon followed, staying with her until they had both found their satisfaction.

He lifted the blanket from his bed and covered her, wrapping it tightly around her before pulling her in close, his chest on her back.

ELLIE ST. CLAIR

"You always smell like roses," he murmured, his nose in the back of her head, and she laughed.

"Rosewater," she explained. "I use it in my bath."

"Then my new life goal shall ensure that all of our houses will be well stocked with the stuff."

She laughed but then became much more subdued.

"Oh, Valentine, your mother is going to hate me."

"She doesn't hate you," he said, knowing his words sounded trite, but they were the truth. "I know it is difficult to tell sometimes, but she acts out of love. She thinks it is in my best interests — and her own — to do what she believes is right. It may take some convincing, but she will see in time that this is what is best for all of us. For me to be happy."

"Valentine?"

"My goodness," Rebecca said as his mother's voice flowed down the hallway. "Your mother certainly has a sixth sense."

Val chuckled. "We'll let her wander for a bit."

"My father..." Rebecca began, unsure of just what to say to Valentine.

"He will live with us, of course," Valentine said, nodding against the back of her head.

"I cannot leave him," Rebecca said, appreciating his words. "But you do know that others may find him mad? Instead of marrying a woman to raise your recognition, you might be marrying one who will bring it down. And Valentine..."

She paused. She had never put her fear into words. It had seemed too selfish to worry about after all that her father had gone through, but if Valentine was prepared to spend his life with her, then he must understand.

"What if, someday... I succumb to whatever is afflicting him?"

Valentine pulled her close. "Then I will be right beside you, helping you along just as you are doing for him. But do

218

not think of it, Rebecca. Whatever comes our way, we'll deal with it, together, one day at a time."

She smiled, tension falling from her as she snuggled back in his arms. For the first time in as long as she could remember, all seemed right in her world.

Even when, a few hours later, she gathered all of her courage and knocked on the door of the drawing room, where Mrs. St. Vincent sat within.

"Enter," came her voice, and Rebecca stepped forward through the door, her heart in her throat.

"Mrs. St. Vincent," she said. "I am glad to find you alone."

Valentine's mother eyed her with a stare but said nothing. Unnerved but determined, Rebecca asked if she could sit, to which Mrs. St. Vincent gave a terse nod.

"Valentine told me that he has informed you of our intentions to marry," she began. She had hidden with Jemima in her laboratory, watching with fascination as her friend mixed chemicals and studied slides underneath a microscope. Rebecca had no idea what she was doing, but it was intriguing to watch her.

"He has," Mrs. St. Vincent said with a nod.

"I—" Rebecca began, but Mrs. St. Vincent held up a hand.

"I must first apologize," Mrs. St. Vincent said, shocking Rebecca into silence. "I said many harsh things to you. I cannot say that I didn't mean some of what I said, but perhaps I went about it in the wrong way. I know I may seem mean and petty, but I truly do always simply want what is best for my children. I had thought for Valentine, that would mean a woman who could guide him around this new world we find ourselves thrust into. But it seems I might have been wrong about that. For when he told me about the two of you, I have quite honestly never seen such happiness on his face before, and that warms a mother's heart."

She looked at Rebecca with some question in her eyes.

"You do know he has no money? You will be receiving a title but nothing more."

"I understand, Mrs. St. Vincent," she said, biting back a smile at the woman's continued defense of her son. "The title means nothing to me, though I will do all I can to best represent the Wyndham title and St. Vincent name. I apologize for deceiving you as well, and I thank you for not sharing my own family's secret."

"Well, I am glad now that I didn't," she said, before looking off into the distance. "This has been both an interesting and yet difficult transition to navigate, Miss Lambert, and I feel that I have done a rather poor job of it. I suppose now it will be new to us all, and the best way forward will be as a united front."

"I completely agree," Rebecca said with a small smile.

"Forgive me?" Mrs. St. Vincent asked, though she maintained her rigid spine and raised chin. Rebecca knew just how difficult it likely was for her to ask such a thing, which made her appreciate the request all the more.

"Of course," she said, rising to leave. "Oh, there is one more thing."

"Yes?"

"I know you would prefer that Valentine give up pugilism as much as I would. But it is part of who he is and we cannot change it. So instead, I think we both must embrace it."

Mrs. St. Vincent stiffened even more so for a moment, before finally relenting. "You know what happened as a result of it?"

"I do. But the fault lies with those who perpetrated such an act, does it not? Since the man is no longer with us, I think there is no longer any blame to spread."

Mrs. St. Vincent didn't seem to entirely agree with Rebecca but, at the very least, she seemed to consider her words. "Very well. I may not like it, but I will hold my tongue."

"Thank you," Rebecca said and, her heart much fuller, took her leave.

Valentine was waiting outside the door.

"Too nervous to join us?" Rebecca asked, arching an eyebrow when she saw him.

"I just thought perhaps you two ladies would appreciate a moment alone."

She punched him in the arm, but he didn't even flinch.

"*That* is how you punch?"

"I'm sorry I am not as highly expert as you."

"Let me show you some proper technique," he said, sweeping his arm out with a flourish. "Right this way. As it so happens, the most wonderful architect I have ever met has built me the most beautiful boxing ring right in my own home…"

Rebecca laughed and followed her soon-to-be-husband down the corridor for her very first boxing lesson.

It was one she would never forget.

EPILOGUE

"*S*tunning."

"Beautiful."

"Classically unique."

"Such an intriguing blend of style."

Rebecca blushed with pleasure each time one of their guests complimented Wyndham House. They were holding their first ball since both the completion of the renovations had been accomplished and she had become the Duchess of Wyndham.

She was terrified on all accounts, but Valentine kept one arm wrapped possessively around her.

Guests flowed in, from earls and marquesses to the boys — now men — Valentine had been raised with in Hungerford. It was an interesting array of people, but it spoke to who Valentine was and the role he had accepted for himself as both the Duke of Wyndham and as Valentine St. Vincent.

"Thank you," he would say to each compliment. "But I must tell you that it is all due to the creativity and ingenuity of my wife. The daughter of Albert Lambert, she has learned from his style and expertise and added her own touch. I cannot wait to see what she does with Stonehall."

Some seemed skeptical, others judgmental, but still others congratulated Rebecca on a job well done.

A few men even complimented Valentine on his latest showing at Jackson's.

"You have much to teach us all!" Lord Epsom said with a chuckle after he and his wife arrived, and Valentine simply nodded gracefully.

"Rebecca!"

She turned with a smile to see that Freddie had arrived, and soon enough the two of them found a moment with Jemima and Celeste. The four of them had developed a regular time for tea each week. It was freeing, to have the opportunity to speak openly about what each of them held a passion for. Rebecca might never fully understand the worlds they each inhabited, but she did her best to follow along.

"Your lottery has been on the tongues of many of the *ton*, Rebecca," Freddie said.

"Not always in the most positive of lights, I imagine," Rebecca said dryly, and Freddie smiled.

"Some say the idea is ingenious and your father is being hailed as a mastermind once again. Others are not entirely pleased about the prospects of just who might move into Mayfair."

"The houses will be given to their prize winners tomorrow," Rebecca said. "It is quite exciting to know that they will finally be lived in. My father's debts are cleared and his good name restored. I am thankful, and of course grateful to Valentine, and to you, Jemima," she said with a smile for her sister-in-law.

"It was your idea," Jemima said. "I simply helped it along."

"Well, I am very glad you did," Rebecca said, but they were

soon interrupted by a young lord who arrived to claim Celeste for a dance. She looked back over her shoulder with regret, but they simply laughed and waved her on.

Valentine was the next to arrive, holding out his hand to Rebecca.

"But we've danced twice already," she said, looking over to her friends for confirmation. "That would be scandalous, would it not?"

"I believe we are past worrying about scandal," he said, wagging his fingers at her, tempting her. "Come, join your husband for a dance."

"Oh, very well," she said, sighing as though it was of extreme trouble, though warmth rushed through her when she placed her hand in his.

"As lovely as this all is," he said, looking around them. "I am much looking forward to my ballroom being empty again, and our home returning to the family."

"Though we will soon be departing for Stonehall," she reminded him, and he nodded, looking at her with speculation. "Our lands are doing well with our new stewards as well as O'Donnell now in place. Perhaps, as early as next year, we can begin some work."

"Really?" she asked, her heart speeding up at the thought. "Oh, that would be lovely. I have some new ideas — a garden spot in particular…"

He laughed as he moved with her in his arms. When they turned to the other side, Rebecca stole a look out of the corner of her eye to where Mrs. St. Vincent and her father were sitting. Wonder upon wonder, Valentine's mother had become quite the guardian of her father. She wasn't sure whether it was that the woman refused to allow anyone to come to know there was a touch of madness in the family, or whether she truly cared for his wellbeing, but she was kind to him all the same, and for that, Rebecca was grateful.

Just before the ball had started, her father had drawn her to the side.

"Rebecca," he had said, wistfulness filling his eyes as he had looked around the grand foyer, where the dome was now ornamented in gold, resembling the sun just as Rebecca had envisioned. "You did a wonderful job on this house."

She had turned to him with surprise.

"Me?"

"You," he had said with a nod, a nostalgic smile crossing his face. "You are a visionary."

Rebecca smiled once more just remembering her father's words of approval, words she never thought she would hear.

"It's funny how life turns out," she commented, and Valentine looked down at her in bemusement.

"What do you mean?"

"Just how our goals and dreams change and become something much greater than ourselves," she said. "And to make them come true, one cannot do it alone."

"No," he agreed, "which makes me very grateful that I have found the greatest partner."

She smiled up at him, hardly able to believe that he was hers, and hers alone, forever more.

"I love you, my pugilist duke," she said.

"And I love you, my architect duchess."

Despite the gasps of those surrounding them at such a display, he bent and placed a brief kiss on her lips.

"Another scandal?" she said with a smile.

"It's what I do best."

"Never stop."

"Not with you."

They smiled together, a promise that would remain between them forever.

THE END

* * *

Dear reader,

I hope you enjoyed reading Rebecca and Val's story! This was a fun one to write, from exploring the many facets of architecture of the era to reading first-hand accounts of boxing matches.

In this story, you met a few of Rebecca's friends, including Freddie. Her story is told in book two of the series. Keep reading for a sneak peek, or you can download it here: Inventing the Viscount.

If you haven't yet signed up for my newsletter, I would love to have you join us! You will receive Unmasking a Duke for free, as well as links to giveaways, sales, new releases, and stories about my coffee addiction, my struggle to keep my plants alive, and how much trouble one loveable wolf-lookalike dog can get into.

www.elliestclair.com/ellies-newsletter

Or you can join my Facebook group, Ellie St. Clair's Ever Afters, and stay in touch daily.

Until next time, happy reading!

With love,
Ellie

* * *

Inventing the Viscount
The Bluestocking Scandals Book Two

Lady Fredericka "Freddie" Ashworth might never marry for love, but she will settle for a marriage of convenience.

When her intended duke marries another, she must find another suitable candidate. She needs a husband she can tolerate who will provide for her and accept her gift of tinkering and skills of designing and woodworking. But where to find such a man?

A chance connection with a childhood acquaintance stirs her interest, for Lord Miles Luxington seems to be exactly the man she is looking for. He may be cold, standoffish, and unfriendly, but she senses there is more to him.

The truth is, his cold exterior has hidden his affliction for the entirety of his life. If the secret was ever revealed, his father would follow through on his threats to ensure the bloodline remained unsullied. When Freddie proposes a courtship, Miles is hesitant, but his desire for her soon overcomes the risk that if she were to discover his secret, he just might lose everything.

Will their marriage become a life of regret, or one of love greater than either of them could ever have imagined?

* * *

AN EXCERPT FROM INVENTING THE VISCOUNT

LONDON, 1820

*L*ady Fredericka Ashworth watched the man she had been supposed to marry waltz off with another woman.

His wife. And her new friend.

She wasn't the least bit jealous.

No, Valentine St. Vincent, Duke of Wyndham, was not the man for her. She had known it the moment she had met him, when she had seen his gaze slide past her and fall upon the woman he would eventually marry.

As it turned out, she and the duke wouldn't have particularly suited — though she would have married him anyway.

"Are you all right?"

Freddie turned her head to the voice of her friend, Miss Jemima St. Vincent, Valentine's sister. While Freddie and the duke did not develop a relationship, she had, at the very least, formed a great friendship with his sister.

"Perfectly fine," Freddie answered, her smile true. "I was

simply thinking about how well everything worked out. Had your brother and I married, he would have been miserable."

Jemima quirked an eyebrow.

"What makes you say that?"

"He is obviously a passionate man, and there was no spark between us. We would have been friends, but nothing more."

"Would *you* have been fine with that?"

"Yes, I would have," Freddie said with conviction, laughing at Jemima's surprised expression. "Friendship is much more than many are lucky enough to have. Besides, he is one of the few men who would have likely put up with my... eccentricities."

"As he does with mine," Jemima murmured, and Freddie nodded.

"Exactly."

Jemima looked around them at her family's ballroom, filled with people who were eager to make the new duchess' acquaintance. Freddie and Jemima were currently hiding in the corner. Jemima's friend, Celeste Keswick, had reluctantly agreed to a dance orchestrated by her mother but would be returning shortly.

"But, Freddie, don't you want *more?*" Jemima asked, her plea impassioned. "Don't you desire love, like Rebecca and Val have found?"

Freddie adamantly shook her head.

"Not at all," she said, setting her chin. "I thought I had it once before. It wasn't worth it."

"Oh Freddie, I had no idea—"

But Freddie smiled sadly and shook her head.

"Another time. Suffice it to say that I would be content with a man who would respect me, be friendly to me, and allow me to do as I please."

"Not a particularly strong man, then?" Jemima asked, to

which Freddie shrugged.

"I suppose you can say that."

"Must you marry at all?" Jemima persisted, to which Freddie nodded sadly.

"If I didn't have to, I wouldn't," she said. "But I am already four-and-twenty. My parents are desperate for me to marry. They will support me for as long as they must, of course, but I know they worry — and rightly so. My sisters are married, and with no brothers, one day my father's title will go to a cousin. I should hardly like to have to place the entirety of my existence on his benevolence — or lack thereof."

"It isn't fair, is it?" Jemima murmured, to which Freddie shook her head.

"Of course not. But that is the reality of our lives, Jemima, so we must make the best of it. Ah, here comes my mother now with a potential beau in tow. She was truly heartbroken when your brother and Rebecca married, you know."

Jemima squinted at the approaching pair. "Who is that with her? We haven't been part of society long enough for me to know many of the *ton* yet."

Freddie craned her neck around the dizzying array of swirling dancers before them. The man beside her mother was only slightly taller than she was, which meant he was rather short himself. Curly reddish-brown hair, trepidation on his face…

"Oh! I'm in luck. It's simply Lord Gilmore."

"What of Lord Gilmore?" Celeste said as she rejoined them, her pale cheeks flushed from the exertion of dancing. "Please don't say my mother is bringing him here for me. I am finished with dancing this evening. Besides, he's nice enough, if a bit of a bore."

"Agreed," Freddie said with a smile. "But no, it is my

mother this time. Our families have known one another for ages. There is nothing particularly disappointing to say about Miles except that he hardly ever speaks and conversing with him is akin to speaking to a statue."

"My brother likes him," Celeste said with a shrug. "I haven't heard many speak ill of him. An agreeable sort. Goes along with everything."

An idea sparked in Freddie's mind — one that Jemima clearly suspected by the intense way she was looking at her.

"You have a rather intriguing look on your face, Freddie," she remarked, and Freddie nodded. Perhaps they could all find what they were looking for — both Freddie, as well as her parents.

There was only one unknown factor.

Miles himself.

* * *

MILES FOLLOWED Lady Rothwell across the ballroom with trepidation. He had no wish to dance with her daughter, but the woman had been insistent. When Lady Rothwell wanted something, well, she was known to chase after it with the stubbornness of a dog after a stick.

When he finally realized that she wasn't going to let him alone without his agreement, he decided he would come and get this over with.

He knew she was chattering incessantly beside him as they walked, but he didn't bother attempting to determine just what she was saying, for he knew her well enough to be aware that her words flew so fast they required a great deal of concentration, and usually it wasn't worth the effort.

Lady Fredericka, on the other hand…

Despite her diminutive size, it was easy to find her

through the crowd. She was as pleasing to the eye as she had always been. The same light-brown hair, the color of cocoa, piled high on her head in the latest style, well-crafted ringlets floating around her temples. The same warm brown eyes, wide in her heart-shaped face. That same knowing, intelligent smile on her pink, bow-shaped lips.

A smile that was currently directed at him. Why did she look so cunning, so satisfied? It slightly unnerved him. He hadn't seen her in a couple of years now, for their paths didn't cross nearly as often as they had as children. He only attended these things to appease his mother, despite the fact that he hated them with all of his being.

The music was too loud, the ballrooms too echoey, and the conversation too difficult.

But his mother was insistent that they attend, that he begin the search for a wife. She was desperate for grandchildren.

And he would do anything for his mother. Without her, who knows where he would be. Likely a madhouse. Instead, he was the Viscount of Gilmore, heir to the Marquess of Dorrington, and no one knew his secret.

He intended to keep it that way, but accompanying ladies such as Lady Fredericka in dances only added to the challenge. What made it worse was he knew her well enough to be aware that she wasn't an empty-headed simpering miss. No, Lady Fredericka was one of the most observant people he knew, and one of the very reasons he attempted to keep his distance from her, despite her beauty.

But here he was.

"Lady Fredericka," he said with a bow before holding out a hand. "Would you care to join me in a dance?"

He looked up at her, awaiting her response.

"Of course, Lord Gilmore," she said with a smile, placing

her hand in his. He led her to the floor, saying nothing else, both relieved and chagrined when a waltz began to play. They were easiest to dance, for he only had to count, but if she decided to have a conversation, it might prove rather difficult.

But, of course, she did. She had always had much to say. He leaned back slightly to determine just exactly what she was now saying.

"How are you enjoying the Season?"

"Just fine," he responded, noticing from up close how much she had grown into her looks. She was still small, but he was struck by the warmth of her brown eyes and her easy smile. She had always been a precocious little thing, but now she had gentled somewhat. "It's been busy."

"I can imagine," she said, before saying something that he didn't quite catch.

"Pardon me?"

"I said that it is good to see you again. It has been so long."

"It has," he said, wishing she would dispense with the polite conversation and allow them to simply dance.

"I believe our fathers are still acquaintances, but it is a shame they do not spend time together as they used to," she said, to which Miles shook his head.

"It is not a shame, Lady Fredericka. You know as well as I do that my father has never been easy to get along with, and it has only worsened as he has aged."

Her eyes widened in shock and her mouth snapped shut. Thank goodness.

Unfortunately, it didn't last.

"How is your mother? She is always such a dear. I have seen her time and again when she comes for tea."

"My mother is well," he said, pleased she had finally found a topic of conversation which he was interested in taking part in. "She especially enjoys visits with your mother. A respite from her own home."

"Yes," she said, blinking but nodding sagely. "I suppose that is true."

"She always liked you, Lady Fredericka."

"Oh, come, Miles, call me Freddie, please. The fact that we have aged is hardly reason for us to become so formal with one another."

"Very well," he said, softening, but then muttered a curse as he stumbled slightly into Freddie when they both stepped forward at the same time. He had become distracted and stopped counting.

"I'm sorry," he apologized, but she shook her head, saying something he didn't quite catch before a smile softened her lips.

"You know, Miles, no one has regarded me so intensely for quite some time."

He swallowed. There was a reason he did so, and it wasn't the same one she had conjectured. She squeezed his hand, which was currently outstretched and wrapped around hers.

"Miles, I must ask you something. Something important."

He nodded.

"Would you— would you call upon me tomorrow?"

Miles lost count altogether at her question. He stopped, blinked, and she, continuing to move, ran right into him. He caught her, holding her up. Had he heard her correctly? She wanted *him* to call upon her? He asked her to repeat herself, which she did. Yes, it seemed he was correct.

"Why?" he said, causing her cheeks to flush beautifully, and then he moved her out of the way before another couple knocked into her.

"Why not?" she asked with a shrug before taking her plump bottom lip between her teeth, worrying it for a moment – causing an unexpected flicker of desire to course through him. "We have known one another long enough to be aware that there is nothing distasteful about the other, no family secrets or skeletons in the cupboard." Or so she thought. "Unless my mother is in the wrong, you require a wife, so you are currently seeking one out, and I am far past the marrying age. I need someone to provide for me. Does that answer your question?"

If he was right, she seemed angry with him, though why, he had no idea. Her reasons for courting were as unromantic as he had ever heard, but perhaps she had a point.

"It's only a call," she said, holding her head high. "It is not as though I am proposing marriage. Yet."

Miles took her hand and led her off the dance floor, needing to be free of the swirling dancers, to go somewhere where he could properly hear her and not have her words garbled by the music.

"Freddie," he said when they were out of the ballroom and into the foyer to where the doors led. "Are you sure about this?"

A frown marred her perfect features.

"Do you not *want* to call upon me? I understand if you do not wish to. Perhaps there is someone else you are—"

"There is no one else."

"It was just a thought, Miles," she said, and he could tell she was attempting to feign nonchalance. "If you'd prefer not to, it is perfectly fine."

He sighed. She had clearly decided that something was the matter with *her*, which was so far from the truth. He was surprised by her lack of confidence.

"All right, Freddie. I'll be there."

"Well, you needn't be so excited about it. You know what — this was a terrible idea."

She moved to brush past, but he grasped her arm and gently turned her toward him.

"I will see you tomorrow," he said firmly. "Goodnight."

It was he who walked past her now. It was time to find his mother, and get the hell out of here.

* * *

FOR MORE, download *Inventing the Viscount,* available on Amazon and through Kindle Unlimited.

ALSO BY ELLIE ST. CLAIR

Discovering the Baron

The Valet Experiment

Writing the Rake

Risking the Detective

A Noble Excavation

A Gentleman of Mystery

The Bluestocking Scandals Box Set: Books 1-4

The Bluestocking Scandals Box Set: Books 5-8

Blooming Brides

A Duke for Daisy

A Marquess for Marigold

An Earl for Iris

A Viscount for Violet

The Blooming Brides Box Set: Books 1-4

Happily Ever After

The Duke She Wished For

Someday Her Duke Will Come

Once Upon a Duke's Dream

He's a Duke, But I Love Him

Loved by the Viscount

Because the Earl Loved Me

Happily Ever After Box Set Books 1-3

Happily Ever After Box Set Books 4-6

The Victorian Highlanders

Duncan's Christmas - (prequel)

Callum's Vow

Finlay's Duty

Adam's Call

Roderick's Purpose

Peggy's Love

The Victorian Highlanders Box Set Books 1-5

Searching Hearts

Duke of Christmas (prequel)

Quest of Honor

Clue of Affection

Hearts of Trust

Hope of Romance

Promise of Redemption

Searching Hearts Box Set (Books 1-5)

Standalones

Always Your Love

The Stormswept Stowaway

A Touch of Temptation

Christmastide with His Countess

Her Christmas Wish

Merry Misrule

A Match Made at Christmas

For a full list of all of Ellie's books, please see

www.elliestclair.com/books.

ABOUT THE AUTHOR

Ellie has always loved reading, writing, and history. For many years she has written short stories, non-fiction, and has worked on her true love and passion -- romance novels.

In every era there is the chance for romance, and Ellie enjoys exploring many different time periods, cultures, and geographic locations. No matter when or where, love can always prevail. She has a particular soft spot for the bad boys of history, and loves a strong heroine in her stories.

Ellie and her husband love nothing more than spending time at home with their children and Husky cross. Ellie can typically be found at the lake in the summer, pushing the stroller all year round, and, of course, with her computer in her lap or a book in hand.

She also loves corresponding with readers, so be sure to contact her!

www.elliestclair.com
ellie@elliestclair.com